WANTED

HOSTAGE RESCUE TEAM SERIES

KAYLEA CROSS

WANTED

Copyright © 2016
by Kaylea Cross

* * * * *

Cover Art & Formatting by
<u>Sweet 'N Spicy Designs</u>

* * * * *

ISBN: 978-1523614424

Dedication

To all the Bauer and Zoe fans out there! This one's for you. Because we could all use more Bauer in our lives, am I right?

Kaylea

Author's Note

Dear readers,

I love my cast of characters in the **HRT** series, but many of you know that Bauer and Zoe are my very favorites (shhh, don't tell the others, I wouldn't want to hurt their feelings!).

I've been wanting to write about these two again, and finally got the chance in *Wanted*. Hope you enjoy the surprises I have in store for you!

Happy reading!

Kaylea Cross

Chapter One

Zoe Renard was the key.

Amanda turned on her laptop and set her fingers on the keyboard, a sharp sense of anticipation humming inside her. Her expertise with IT meant she had a certain skillset that was highly sought after. Now she was finally using that proficiency to get what she wanted.

What she *deserved*. And by the time anyone managed to trace her accounts and figure out who she was, she'd have disappeared.

While Zoe hadn't been her original target, she was a means to an end. A convenient one. And even though Amanda had suppressed that instinct for a long time, she didn't have to anymore. Because now she finally had the motivation and the means to act on what her gut had been telling her all along.

Zoe had to die.

Her heart beat faster as she typed out her latest

message, this one the most blatant of all. Screw being subtle. She wanted Zoe to be scared when she read this one, wanted her to feel like something was coming.

Because it was. And sooner than she realized.

A fierce sense of satisfaction curled inside her as her fingers tapped the keys. Her entire plan for the cushy future she'd mapped out for herself had come raining down around her in fiery ruins because of Zoe. Now she was going to make that nosy Goth bitch pay.

Except finding her was proving a challenge, even for Amanda.

Since shacking up with her FBI agent lover after what she'd gone through last year, Zoe kept a low profile these days. Amanda had been unable to find an address for her so far, and even after tracking credit card purchases and the like, she'd been forced to resort to stalking her pen name through various social media sites online.

Fucking weird, the way she liked to dress up like something out of a Tim Burton movie. The woman owned a whole wardrobe of creepy Victorian outfits, had ridiculous, freaky-colored hair and heavy black eye makeup. And her writing was even more bizarre than her physical appearance.

For some reason Amanda would never understand, a surprising number of people seemed to love Zoe's books, and how she made her characters suffer in the pages of her romantic horror novels. The woman had a dark and twisted imagination to match that carefully cultivated queen-of-darkness image, especially when it came to torturing the people she wrote about.

Amanda wished she could do the same to her. Show her how it was done in real life.

The thought triggered a flash of inspiration in her brain.

"That's perfect," she whispered under her breath,

goose bumps rising on her arms as she deleted what had been there and wrote the new words. The new message fit the escalation of the previous e-mails nicely too. Made it seem like Zoe's stalker was becoming increasingly unhinged.

I knew as soon as I read your first book that you were like me. You love to inflict pain, take pleasure in it. A fellow sadist. Wouldn't you like to know how it feels to suffer the way your characters do? I think I'm going to enjoy doing it to you. Carve you up just like your character Drake did to his victims...

She let the threat trail off there, knowing it would be more intense that way. After studying the message for a few moments longer, she decided it had just the right tone she wanted and hit Send.

"And now we wait," she murmured to herself, pulling her cat into her lap to stroke its silky fur. His rumbling purr was soothing in the quiet, cozy apartment she'd been renting for the past few weeks. The longest she'd stayed in one place since leaving her job and starting down the path to freedom.

In just a few short days it would all be over, this year-long path she'd been traveling. Zoe would report the threat immediately to the cops and the FBI. That should trigger enough activity through the various sites and accounts Amanda was monitoring for her to get enough intel to figure out where Zoe was.

"Has to be close to Quantico," she said to her cat, who closed his eyes and swished his tail in response. That's where the FBI's Hostage Rescue Team was based. And Amanda wanted the offered reward money badly enough that she'd even contemplated going on base to do her recon.

But there was a difference between being desperate and just being plain stupid. So she'd chosen the safer option of going after Zoe instead.

Amanda wanted that money. She *needed* the money, and the sense of satisfaction she would get from having a part in this operation.

Not long now…

Zoe was the reason Carlos had died. The reason she was now forced to take these drastic and risky measures. It would be worth it in the end though.

Soon Amanda would have both her revenge and the money she needed to start a new life in the tropical paradise she'd been dreaming of, escape there once she got the reward money.

She turned off the laptop, a sly smile curving her mouth. It felt good to finally be back in control after months of uncertainty and looking over her shoulder every moment. Everything was ready now. Her only regret was that she wouldn't be able to savor Zoe's fearful expression when she realized she had another potentially deadly problem on her hands.

Once they got Zoe, her lover would come for her. Then they'd both die.

****

FBI Special Agent Clay Bauer snapped out of a light doze when the captain announced they'd be landing soon. Considering everything his team had just gone through, the long-ass flight from Anchorage back to northern Virginia had given them some welcome time to decompress.

Now all he could think about was Zoe, and how close he was to seeing her again. He'd missed his Goth goddess like crazy these past few weeks. There was no one else like his raven; she was a unique and complicated mix of brilliant and driven, imaginative and dark. She could be sharp-tongued at times, she was independent and fiercely loyal. Lucky for him, she was also incredibly loving.

He flat-out worshipped her, thanked his lucky stars every day that she'd somehow seen past his grim exterior and decided she wanted him anyway.

Next to him his commander, Supervisory Special Agent Matt DeLuca let out a yawn and stretched his arms over his head with a grunt.

"Looking forward to being in my own bed tonight. Been a long couple of days."

Clay grunted. "Tell me about it." Though DeLuca was most likely looking forward to crawling into bed next to his girlfriend, Briar, just as Clay couldn't wait to do the same with Zoe. It'd been almost three weeks since he'd last been home, and after this latest op he and the others were exhausted. All of them were anxious to get back to Quantico, but he suspected mostly because their women were there waiting for them.

"That was definitely one for the books, huh?" DeLuca muttered.

"Yeah."

He knew Zoe had been worried about him, with all the media coverage about their recent op. Two nights ago they'd taken a cruise ship under the control of a deadly terrorist cell. It had been one scary-ass op, and they'd been lucky not to lose anyone when so many passengers and crew had been killed. The carnage had been staggering.

"Out of all of us, I think Cruzie and Vance are gonna need the downtime the most this week," DeLuca continued.

Clay grunted again and glanced over his left shoulder to look for them. They were sitting together a couple rows back, their shoulders touching as they dozed in their seats, Vance's right arm bandaged tight across his chest. The former SF soldier had wrecked his shoulder while being hoisted into the helo off the ship's deck, and they didn't know when he'd be operational again.

He turned back to DeLuca, who was adjusting his San Diego Chargers cap on his head. "We got anything scheduled once we get back to HQ, or…?" He was really hoping his commander would say no.

"Other than doing inventory and getting everything squared away, no. Not now that the cell responsible for the attack has been dismantled."

Thank God. He didn't think he could take another meeting right now, not when he was so close to seeing Zoe again. Things between them were great—better than great—except he couldn't shake the gut feeling that something had been bothering her the past couple months.

She hadn't said anything, which in and of itself made him concerned. Zoe wasn't exactly known for holding back when she had something on her mind. But his gut told him she was doing just that and he didn't know why.

The plane circled twice then began its final approach. When it parked at the gate all of them stood up to stretch their legs and grab their gear. Clay hefted his ruck and waited in line in the aisle behind DeLuca to offload, aware of a dull ache in his lower back. The surgery he'd undergone to repair a ruptured disk had helped reduce his pain significantly, but it would never go away completely and sitting his ass on a plane for that long didn't help.

From the airfield they drove back to base at Quantico and filed into headquarters to unload their equipment, then showered and changed. By the time Clay grabbed his keys from his locker and called Zoe to tell her he'd be there soon, anticipation tingled in his veins. He was anxious to hear that sweet and slightly husky Louisiana-accented voice.

She didn't answer though. It was dinnertime, so maybe she was cooking or out grabbing something. He slid his phone into his pocket and headed for the door, anxious to get home to surprise her.

On top of some asshole bothering her online she'd

been sick with a bad cold all week and he felt badly that he hadn't been home even one night to help take care of her. He had a feeling his relentless schedule was maybe part of the reason she'd seemed a little less happy lately.

His job demanded a lot of sacrifices from both of them, and though Zoe was fully supportive of his career, he could understand why even someone as strong as her might be feeling neglected right now. Clay intended to spend lots of quality time with her over the next few days to try and make up for his absence.

But at the door leading out to the parking lot, a voice from behind stopped him.

"Can I talk to you for a sec?" a familiar Alabama drawl asked.

Clay turned to face his team leader and best friend, who also happened to be Zoe's cousin. That's how they'd met in the first place. Tuck tipped his dark blond head toward an office just down the hallway.

Disguising his irritation, Clay nodded, because Tuck wouldn't ask to talk to him privately unless it was important. "Sure, yeah." He followed him inside the empty room, wondering what was going on. Why the need for privacy?

Tuck flipped on the lights and shut the door before facing him, hands on hips. "So, Celida and I are getting married on Saturday."

Whoa. Clay's eyebrows shot up. "As in, five days from now?" They'd been engaged for a year now, so why the huge rush all of a sudden?

He nodded, looking tired. Clay knew the weight of responsibility of being team leader weighed heavily on his friend, even if Tuck would never say it. He held himself personally accountable for his guys and anything that happened to them. Clay thought that all of them coming home alive after this latest op should be evidence enough that Tuck had done his job, but the guy was notoriously hard on himself.

They all were. It's what kept them sharp, what made them all keep striving to improve as operators and made them one of the best counter-terrorism units in the world.

"Yeah. We've set a date twice before and it's fallen through both times because shit just keeps getting in the way, so we're just gonna get 'er done before something else comes up. Besides, as of tomorrow the team's officially on training cycle, so it should work out. We decided on it last night, figured we shouldn't wait."

"Okay." Made sense. Between Tuck and Celida's crazy work schedules with the FBI, they didn't get much time to themselves, let alone time to plan out something like a wedding.

"This last op hit home for me," Tuck admitted. "If I'd been KIA, Celida would have gotten nothing except what I've detailed in my will. No benefits, no nothing, because we're not married. I want to marry her, yeah, but I also want to make sure she's protected if anything happens to me. So it's gonna be this weekend."

The words hit home. Hard. Clay knew they were the truth, and he'd thought the same things about Zoe lately. Virginia law didn't recognize couples living together as having a common law marriage. As of right now, she was unprotected too, and it bothered him.

Good thing he was already planning to rectify that. "I hear you."

"So you'll stand up for me?"

As in, best man? As in, wearing a suit up there at the front of the church or whatever in front of everyone? He mentally scowled. "Uh, sure, man. I'd be happy to."

Weddings weren't exactly his favorite thing, not after having gone through a disastrous marriage and an even more disastrous divorce, but that was his own baggage so he'd deal, and suck it up for Tuck. And he couldn't deny he'd been spending a lot of time lately thinking about how he should propose to Zoe.

But she was a freaking romance author, wrote that kind of stuff for a living, so he had to make it both romantic and memorable. He wanted it to be a perfect moment she'd cherish for the rest of her life. Something that would catch her off guard and be unique, something sentimental.

No pressure.

Thankfully, the idea of getting married again didn't make him feel strangled or suffocated the way it would have a year ago. That was Zoe's doing. She made him feel loved and accepted and respected, even admired.

Basically, he was one lucky bastard, to have a woman like her. At least he knew it, tried to love her the way she deserved. Though part of him would probably always feel like she deserved better than being with a hardass like him. It was time for him to man up and do right by her.

Tuck smiled and slapped him on the shoulder. "Good. Don't worry, it's gonna be small, just us four, an official and maybe the rest of the guys if they want to come as guests. Celida already asked Zoe to stand up with her back when we got engaged."

"Yeah, I know." Zoe had been thrilled. She hadn't mentioned anything about the wedding when he'd called last night though. "Does she know it's happening this weekend?"

"Doubt it. Lida's been busy wrapping up the investigation in Anchorage and Seattle and she's been swamped with meetings for the past couple days. She's not flying home until tomorrow night, so I'm going to set everything up."

Clay kept his expression neutral. "*You're* going to plan everything?" Didn't the bride-to-be usually go into full-on control freak mode about stuff like that? Clay's ex-wife sure had. He'd learned real fast to let her do her thing without consulting him.

Tuck shrugged one broad shoulder. "Gonna try. Can't be that tough, we're not even booking a church. All I have to do is find an official and pick a spot to exchange our vows, then get a caterer. Celida said she'll handle all the little stuff once she gets home."

Clay had trouble imagining his badass, former-Delta team leader doing that kind of shit, but whatever. "Okay, well, good luck with that. Do I need a suit?"

"Yeah, a tux. I'll reserve one for you when I go in for mine. It's on my honeydo list." He held up his phone with a wry smile.

A tux. Clay fought the urge to make a face. He hated them with a passion, but when he thought about it, he realized there was one definite bonus for putting up with a few hours of discomfort, in addition to making his buddy happy.

Zoe had a secret suit fetish.

Maybe it was a writer thing but she'd actually come up with a term for it. Suit porn. And the last time he'd worn one for her as part of an elaborate and insanely hot seduction scheme he'd snagged from a scene out of one of her novels—damn, was that really almost a year ago now?—she'd been extremely...enthusiastic in her response.

He couldn't help but grin at the memory. One of the greatest nights of his life.

It continually amazed him that he'd found her, that a woman as beautiful and incredible as Zoe had somehow fallen in love with him, and she even loved his dominant side in bed. Huge bonus, since he didn't have to temper his rough-edged desires around her.

He'd moved into her condo with her soon after the suit porn episode, and things were still great between them all these months later. Before her, he'd never imagined a loving relationship like that was even possible for him, let alone actually being *in* one.

So yeah, he could definitely handle being in a tux for a few hours. Because once the wedding was over, it wouldn't stay on him long.

"What's that leer on your face about?" Tuck asked.

He killed the smile. "Nothing. So you'll keep me posted then? Tell me where I'm supposed to be and when I'm supposed to be there and whatever?" With any luck there wouldn't be a rehearsal dinner or anything.

"Pretty much, yeah."

"Wait, what about a bachelor party?" Wasn't that a best man thing? Because that he could handle. Paintball or dirt biking up in the mountains, a campfire out in the woods afterward and a few cases of beer.

Tuck cocked his head. "Really? You'd set that up for me?"

"Hell yeah, man. Just tell me what day and I'll make it happen." They guys would love it, especially after this latest mission. They needed to blow off steam in the worst way.

He laughed. "I appreciate it."

Clay shifted his stance, fought the urge to check his watch. Was Zoe home yet? Or finished with whatever she'd been doing when he called? "Cool. So, we done here?"

"Yeah. Go ahead, man. Go home to Zoe while I go to my empty house," Tuck said with a grin.

Don't have to tell me twice.

He headed out to his truck, unable to wipe the smile off his face. In less than half an hour from now he'd be walking through his front door. And a minute or two after that, if she was feeling up to it, he planned to have Zoe naked and underneath him on the nearest flat surface.

His phone buzzed with an incoming text. His heart jumped, expecting it to be from Zoe, but it was from a shop he'd visited over a month ago.

Your design is ready.

Perfect, he thought with a smile. He could swing by there tomorrow and have a look at what the jeweler had come up with.

Pulling out of the parking lot, he was already thinking about what he would do to Zoe once he got her naked. They'd been together long enough that he knew exactly what made her hot, what made her beg, and they had a lot of lost time to make up for.

He needed to lock Zoe down. She was definitely The One and deserved better than just being his girlfriend. She'd been more than patient with him over the past year, letting him deal with his own relationship hang-ups without pressuring him for more. He trusted her, owed her far more than that, wanted to give her the security and protection she deserved as his partner.

Because there was no way he wanted to contemplate the prospect of going through life without her.

Chapter Two

Z oe struggled up through the weight of a deep sleep when the mattress shifted. She lifted heavy eyelids and blinked at the fading light streaming through the open blind in the window beside the bed.

A large hand settled next to her face. Her heart jumped but before she could react a familiar, masculine scent mixed with soap registered, then a warm, heavy weight settled against her back.

She relaxed, a sleepy smile curving her mouth. *Clay.*

"You're home," she murmured, stretching like a contented cat beneath him. He was a big boy, his body honed to muscular perfection from hours in the gym and his constant training with the team. Just the feel of him made her stresses melt away. It'd been way too long since she'd felt his arms around her, and this latest mission had scared the hell out of her.

He made a low sound of acknowledgement and lowered his head to nuzzle her nape with his face, his whiskers scratching her skin pleasantly. He must not have shaved for a few days. "Yeah." The large hand next to her face lifted and curved around her forehead, as if checking her temperature. "You still sick? It's not even eight yet."

"Just tired." Exhausted, actually. That cold from hell apparently wasn't done with her yet, because it was still kicking her ass. For the better part of four days she'd lain in bed, using up more than three boxes of tissues until she'd been able to start breathing through her nose again. Only one nostril at a time, of course, never both at the same time.

"I'm so glad you're home safe." She tried to roll over but he stilled her and proceeded to trail kisses across her cheek, down to her jaw, the corner of her mouth. She turned her face away at the last second, before he touched her lips. "I want to kiss you, but I don't want to give you whatever I had."

"I'll work around it," he whispered against her skin, making her grin.

"Good thing you're an expert at adapting on the fly." He was an expert at a *lot* of things, and it continually amazed her. He could fix damn near anything, was way more observant than even she'd realized... And his areas of expertise also extended to how to drive her body wild.

"Hmmm." He cupped the underside of her jaw in his hand, his tongue stroking along the side of her neck, making her shiver. "You miss me, raven?"

The pet name was like another caress, a term of affection he'd first used to acknowledge her love of the macabre and all things Goth. He'd even started calling her that before he'd seen the raven's wings tattooed across the base of her spine.

"*Yes.*" So much. Especially after finding out about what had happened on that cruise ship the other night. It always scared her, to know something terrible could happen to him when he went to work, even if it was just a training op.

Seeing the news coverage on TV had been terrifying

until he'd called her afterward, and the sound of that deep voice on the other end of the phone had finally eased the vise of worry that had been tightening around her chest with every passing hour without any word from him. Her best friend and FBI agent Celida had been out of town and didn't answer her calls, so she'd actually wound up calling Taya, Schroder's girlfriend, instead.

Best decision she could have made. The woman was amazingly calm and resilient, exactly what Zoe had needed in that moment.

She sighed at the feel of Clay's open mouth on her skin. She was tingling all over, already getting wet for him and he'd barely touched her. Her entire body ached for his touch. Right now she wanted to push the whole world away, all her worry, and just focus on this.

She arched into his hand as he trailed his fingers down her throat, his big body shifting slightly to the side so he could reach down and cup one of her breasts. Instantly she flinched and sucked in a breath.

He froze, his big hand cradling her tender flesh. "Sore again already?"

She nodded, letting her eyes drift close. "Yeah." She generally got really sore boobs about a week before her period. "So they're very sensitive."

He made a sound of approval and nipped a tendon at the back of her neck, a scrape of teeth that made her shiver. "Then I'll have to take extra care with them."

The care he took with her always made her melt. Clay was a huge guy, outweighing her by nearly a hundred pounds, and he had a healthy appetite for sex that was dominant and a little rough but the way he touched her was always so perfect. He made her feel safe, wanted and cherished in a way that made her crave him with every cell in her being. He was her addiction and Zoe couldn't get enough.

She arched her back to press her breast into his hand

and tipped her head to the side. The man knew exactly how to make her hot and he was using that insider knowledge now, every caress and kiss turning her boneless, drugging her with desire.

A gentle pinch to her nipple and she gasped, the bundle of nerves so sensitive it was a mix of pleasure and pain. But the pleasure won out, a bright streamer of heat shooting down to between her legs.

He murmured something against her shoulder and kept teasing the rigid center, even as he rolled her onto her stomach and used his heavy thighs to part hers. The heat of his erection seared her damp folds, his free hand slipping beneath her to cup her aching sex. She moaned at the contact and parted her legs wider for him.

A growl of pure male satisfaction reverberated in his chest, vibrating against her back. "Mmmm, my baby definitely missed me." There was no mistaking the pride and approval in his voice, but she was already too far-gone to answer.

She managed a nod, almost beyond the ability to form a coherent thought. He always did this to her. Made her lose control, took her to a place where she couldn't think, could only feel, turned her into a desperate, greedy animal until the only thing she cared about was reaching the release he could give her.

And he always made sure she got there.

Those knowing, callus-roughened fingers were so gentle on her slick flesh, sliding along the throbbing bundle of nerves in an endless caress that had her writhing and moaning. His low chuckle brushed against her jaw, his hands taking her to the brink of madness while his cock teased her opening.

It was too much. She'd gone too long without him.

"*Clay.*" She pushed up hard, trying to scramble up onto her forearms and knees but he kept her pinned beneath him and teased her until she was ready to beg.

She had no pride where he was concerned. With him she was totally free to express her sexuality in whatever way felt good and she loved it when he took control, which he almost always did. Her trust in him was absolute.

"I'm so close," she gasped out, trembling all over. It always stunned her, how fast he took her to the brink. "Do it." The nipple he was tormenting was still tender, but the tiny bite of pain combined with the pleasure only intensified the sensations streaking through her. She wanted him inside her. *Needed* it.

"I want to hear you when you come," he ordered in a low voice, easing his weight forward to press the head of his cock inside her.

There was no way she could stay quiet and he knew it. Her mouth opened on a cry of pure need and she pushed back with her hips, trying to drive him inside her.

"My greedy raven," he murmured, his pleased tone telling her he loved how she let him see her need. She *was* greedy with him. How could she not be, when he made her body feel like this?

One hand cupping her breast and the other buried between her legs, he surged forward in a single thrust that lodged him deep inside her. The sudden stretching and fullness was so intense she gasped.

Her hands gripped the bedding, needing something to hold onto. A choked sob came out of her and as the sensation swamped her she went mindless, her body acting all on its own, hips churning, hungrily going after the release hovering just out of reach.

Clay lowered more of his weight onto her, restricting her movements, and the sensation of being trapped heightened the experience. The muscles in her belly and thighs pulled tight. His fingers toyed with her sensitive bud as he began a slow, deliberate rhythm in and out of her aching core. His big body surrounded her, enveloped her, his size and strength yet another huge turn-on.

Flat on her stomach, pinned by his weight like this, she felt protected, overwhelmed, and she'd missed him so damn much…

His hips pumped slow and firm, fingers caressing her most sensitive spots until the pleasure exploded inside her. Her cries of release echoed in her own ears as the orgasm punched through her, exquisite pulse after pulse rushing through her body.

Behind her Clay growled low in his throat and thrust harder, faster until she felt him swell impossibly thicker inside her. The hand cradling her breast tightened and he buried his face in the nape of her neck as his entire body shuddered, a raw groan of ecstasy ripping out of him.

Weak with pleasure, Zoe melted back into the mattress, savoring the feel of his weight anchoring her, the way his body heat seemed to soak into her bones. "Love you," she murmured, suddenly too tired to even keep her eyes open.

"Love you back." He kissed her cheek, withdrew and slowly rolled off her despite her protests, then curled up behind her and tucked her into the curve of his body, her back to his chest, his thighs cradling hers.

Sleepily she trailed her fingers over one of his forearms, exploring the ropey muscles and tendons there. She would never get tired of touching him. He'd opened up so much emotionally since they'd been together. Not easy for him, after the disaster that had been his relationship with his ex-wife, but every day their bond grew stronger because he trusted Zoe completely.

She kept hoping that one day soon he'd put his old fears behind him for good and ask her to marry him. "I'm glad you're okay. That one was scary."

"Yeah, it was intense. Missed you." He squeezed her tight.

Losing him would gut her. But it also annoyed her to

know that if something had happened to him, legally she'd have had absolutely no say in his medical care or anything else. That wouldn't change unless they got married.

She desperately wanted to, but she wasn't sure if he'd ever be ready to do that again so she'd been careful not to bring it up, not wanting to pressure him for fear he'd retreat emotionally from her. The only thing she'd ever kept silent about in their relationship. Normally she wasn't one to hold back if she had something to say.

They'd been together a year now though. If he didn't want to marry her by now, he probably never would.

Part of her was afraid to ask because she feared she might not like the answer.

He squeezed her tighter. "Cruzie's mom and sister were on board, too."

Zoe gasped and tried to roll over to face him, only managed to get her head turned. "You serious?"

He nodded, those vivid blue eyes steady, dark hair trimmed short. Such a beautiful man. "They're both okay now though."

"Thank God for that." She rolled back over to face the window, let out a sigh of contentment. "You feel good."

"You too." He smoothed her hair away from her forehead. "You're still pretty tired, huh?"

"I just need a full night's sleep, I think." But the heaviness of this exhaustion was starting to worry her a little. Maybe she had mono or something. The stress of the online stalker situation wasn't helping matters.

Maybe now that Clay was home she'd actually be able to go into a deep sleep without worrying some maniac was plotting to come after her. "If I don't feel better by tomorrow I'll call my doctor."

"Okay." He stroked his fingertips over the back of her hand, his touch so gentle, at odds with his size and often grim exterior. "Need anything? Some soup maybe?"

She smiled. He was so sweet with her, her gruff and sexy badass. "No, I'm good. This is all I need." For now, anyway.

He was quiet for a minute, both of them enjoying the sense of closeness. "Any more weird messages in the past couple days?" he finally asked.

"A few, yeah. Haven't checked my e-mails since this morning though, so there could be more." She'd been getting odd messages on her pseudonym's social media sites from a guy online that raised red flags for her. About a dozen so far over the past two weeks. She'd blocked him and he kept using new accounts to contact her.

It had gone from weird to annoying and now past that into cray-cray town. Whoever he was, the guy was purposely trying to creep her out. Clearly he was mentally ill, but something in her gut told her he might be dangerous, and that worried her the most.

Having been stalked and kidnapped once already, she had no desire to ever go through it again, and wanted this situation defused before it escalated. "I didn't want to bug Celida about it again, given what was going on in Seattle and Anchorage."

"I already talked to DeLuca about it, but give them to me in the morning and I'll pass them on to Rycroft."

Alex Rycroft, a higher-up at the NSA Clay had met on the job. "You sure?"

He snorted. "Am I sure I want to take your safety seriously? Yeah. Rycroft has all kinds of resources for that sort of thing at his disposal. And he's a good guy. He'll look into it. His people will be able to trace the IP address in no time."

"All right." Already feeling better about it, thrilled to have Clay home and cuddling her like this, she covered her mouth and let a yawn so big it made her eyes water.

"By the way, did you know Tuck and Celida are

getting married this weekend?"

At that her eyes popped wide open and she half turned toward him. "What? No."

"Yeah. This Saturday, if all goes well. Tuck asked me to stand up for him."

Zoe was a little annoyed that her cousin and best friend hadn't called to tell her themselves, but given that things had been crazy the past few days, she would cut them some slack. She lay back down, snuggled under the covers. "I guess I'd better dig out my bridesmaid dress and see if it still fits." She'd bought it last fall when Celida had bought her wedding gown.

Clay grunted. "Tuck's handling all the details for now. He thinks Celida might not be home for another couple days maybe."

"Really? I'll help him until she gets here, if he wants a hand."

"I'm sure he'd appreciate it. I'm gonna set up some sort of bachelor party thing. You gonna do a shower or whatever?"

She hadn't thought about it because there hadn't been a firm date nailed down before now. Celida wasn't close with her remaining family and Zoe was pretty much her only close girlfriend, but she knew most of the HRT girls and liked them.

It was rare that they all got together outside of team functions, so that would be nice. And right now all but one of them were only girlfriends rather than wives, which helped them bond and feel less like outsiders.

"I'll do something." Zoe wanted to plan something relaxing but special for her. Hopefully tomorrow she'd feel more like herself again.

"Okay. Figured you would." Clay kissed the top of her head, his breath ruffling her hair slightly. "Sleep now, baby."

"Yeah." Secure in his embrace, she closed her eyes

but couldn't shake the feeling of dread about finding another message from her online tormenter in the morning.

****

Amanda was up early monitoring the e-mail accounts she'd been watching for the past few weeks when the call came in. She didn't recognize the number, waited for the caller to leave a message.

Once she confirmed it was Dominic, she called him back using a burner phone. "Where are you?"

"I'm on my way from the hotel. I'll be there in twenty minutes."

"*No.*" She absolutely didn't want him in her place.

The rent here was pricey for a reason, because the security was state-of-the-art. She didn't want anyone on the security staff to see him on video surveillance and be able to link the two of them together after the fact. Once this op was over she needed to make a clean getaway out of the country and wouldn't risk leaving threads to tangle her up.

"I'll meet you someplace, but tomorrow, because I'm working right now. Have you got everything?" He was supposed to have picked up his weapons and gear before he checked into the hotel.

"Yes." He sounded pissed off at her demanding attitude, but she didn't care. He might be the one who would take the actual shots when the time came, but she'd set this whole thing up and had done all the work. He was lucky she was giving him as much of the reward money as she was, for two pulls of the trigger.

"I'm getting close," she told him without going into specifics. Zoe had definitely received her last message because the chatter Amanda had been monitoring had mentioned it early this morning.

And Zoe was worried enough that someone had apparently contacted the NSA on her behalf. There'd also been zero activity on her social media accounts in the past two days, something unusual that Amanda found very interesting.

Oh yeah, the bitch was scared.

"I should have her location by tomorrow afternoon." Maybe sooner, if she was lucky.

Because she liked to fly her freak flag high and proud, Zoe stood out wherever she went. Amanda had been studying her credit card records, had found a few patterns that gave her key places to check. Getting security footage on her own was possible, but she'd already maxed out her favors with her existing contacts.

Working by herself, it was easier to go and stake a handful of places out. Zoe's favorite coffee shop was a good place to start. "I'll call you once I know something more."

"What's your deal with her, anyway? The reward is for one of the HRT guys, not their women," he said, his voice filled with disdain.

As if targeting a woman was beneath him—a newbie enforcer for one of the Fuentes cartel's only surviving lieutenants. She was taking a huge risk by enlisting the help of an enforcer with a short track record but time was limited and she'd had few options.

"It's personal, and don't worry about it because I've told you before, she's the weak link. If we get her and wait, he'll come to us." Targeting an HRT member was difficult and downright dangerous, but getting to them through someone else without training was doable. As a soft, civilian target, Zoe would be an easy enough mark once Amanda got a lock on her location.

"Is it because of what happened with Ruiz?" he pressed.

The mention of the name gave her pause. How did

he even know about Carlos?

Maybe she hadn't been in love with Carlos Ruiz at first, but he'd been useful, good in bed when she'd traded sex for information, and the connections and intel he'd given her had proven lucrative. Given all that, it wasn't surprising that she'd fallen for him completely within a few months. She'd loved him single-mindedly, would have done anything for him.

It hadn't been until weeks later that she'd found out he'd been fucking around on her. He'd been obsessed with getting back together with his ex, Leticia, and it had been his undoing. Then he'd kidnapped Zoe when she'd interfered with his plan, the HRT had killed him during her rescue, and Amanda's world had come tumbling down around her.

She'd been lost after he died. Just as lost as when her mother had drunk herself to death and she'd been bounced from foster home to foster home afterward at the age of nine.

No one had wanted her. Not really, throughout her entire life. Until Carlos.

With Carlos she'd truly believed they'd have a future together. He'd once promised her a beach house in the Caribbean, where they'd spend their days enjoying the warm trade winds that rustled through the fronds of the coconut palms outside.

Whenever things got too hard, when despair threatened to drown her, that's what she thought of. She no longer dreamed of sharing that life with Carlos, but she would damn well take her revenge on Zoe and get the reward money to buy that house for herself.

"Let me rephrase so it's crystal clear," she told Dom. "My deal with her is none of your goddamn business. I hired you to do this job, and you agreed to the terms. It's too late to walk now."

If he tried, or if he thought he could turn her in

afterward and take all the money, she would bury him. As insurance she had enough evidence saved up on him to put him away for two consecutive life sentences. He wouldn't dare cross her.

"Well then let me be clear, *sweetheart*," he sneered back. "This line of work is new to you, so let me help you out. You gotta keep a clear head, leave emotions at the door. Understand? Otherwise you get killed. Simple as that."

His attitude rankled. "I'm not stupid." Desperate maybe, but definitely not stupid. No, she'd planned this all out carefully.

"And how do you know we'll even get the money after this? Fuentes is in lockdown. How are you gonna even prove it was us?"

"I already told you, I have insider sources." Handy contacts she'd developed at her previous job. Until his capture several months ago, Fuentes—who Carlos had done side jobs for—had been the head of the most formidable drug cartel in the United States.

And he still had power. Even from within the walls of one of the most secure prisons in the country, he was pulling strings. She didn't know how exactly, and didn't care. All she cared about was the money he was offering.

A million dollars for a hit on one of the FBI's Hostage Rescue Team members. A metaphorical middle finger to the men who had put him behind bars and killed several of his best enforcers.

That money would be *hers*.

Dom grunted. "I don't do business with women for a reason. They're too emotional, and that shit causes nothing but problems."

Amanda almost laughed out loud at that. Carlos was the only person she'd ever loved. "You'd be the first person to ever accuse me of being emotional," she said dryly.

Cold, maybe. Others had called her detached, but that just made it easier for her to get what she wanted. Lack of conscience made a lot of things so much easier. She'd do this job, take the money and sleep like a baby once she was safe in the Caribbean.

After everything she'd gone through in her life, she *deserved* that much.

She swallowed her annoyance and went for reasonable. "Whether we like it or not, we're a team for now. You do your job, I'll do mine. Let's leave it at that." She didn't trust him, but she needed him. Although she had some weapons training, it was preschool level compared to what Dominic had learned as a sniper with the military.

He made a disparaging sound. "Just call me when you find her."

The call disconnected before she could respond.

Amanda slapped her phone down on the table with a muttered, "Go fuck yourself."

She took a breath, cleared her head. Their alliance was fragile and uneasy enough without adding any more animosity between them. Besides, she had more important things to focus on right now, or there wouldn't be an op to plan.

Pulling up the file she'd created, she narrowed down her final choices to stake out and selected the one that made the most sense. An average of five times per week, Zoe stopped in at a specific coffee shop about fifteen minutes from Quantico.

In the morning Amanda would drive there and stake it out. If Zoe showed, she'd follow her, all day if necessary, and find out where she lived. If she could just track her down once, from there it should be easy enough to come up with a plan and for Dominic to figure out where he wanted to set up for the shot.

She sighed and rubbed at her temples, the beginnings

of a headache throbbing there. Things had been so much easier for her when Carlos had been alive.

The truth was he'd lied to her and used her, sure, but she'd always come out ahead in their relationship. When he died, everything had become so much harder. She'd had no choice but to leave her job and the steady pay it brought, because internal affairs had begun sniffing around, asking questions about her alleged relationship with him.

No one knew she'd been in love with him. Not even Carlos.

It had taken her months afterward to earn the trust of one of the Fuentes cartel's top lieutenants. She'd taken a few bribes from Alvarez prior to leaving her job, and once earned triple her pitiful government salary from a single favor to him. So her next decision had been a no-brainer.

With nowhere to go and no one to turn to after the agency began investigating her, she'd gone to her contacts in the drug cartel. After worming her way into Alvarez's circle and becoming one of his lovers, she'd lived the good life for a little while.

Then Zoe's HRT boyfriend and his team had killed Alvarez too, costing Amanda the sugar daddy she'd so carefully cultivated in an attempt to salvage her dream of becoming independently wealthy.

Rage and resentment built inside her, slowly eating at her like acid. She never wanted to be someone's whore ever again. She was sick of her shitty life, of having to spread her legs for various cartel members, and before that, her foster father, just to have some security.

No more. She had vowed to herself that she would get enough money to ensure she'd never have to trade her body for anything again.

In her life within the cartel she'd been well on her way to becoming independently wealthy in her own right, even if it came with a heavy price. With Fuentes's entire network either dead, captured or on the run, her only option now was to enlist Dom's help to get this reward money and start over out of the country.

No one was taking that chance from her. She was ready do whatever it took to make this happen. It was time for her to take control and go after what she wanted. A new life and a fresh start far away from here.

Everything went back to Zoe, and her lover. "They've both got this coming," she muttered to herself, a wave of anger suffusing her. She'd worked hard to get where she'd been, and they'd destroyed it all.

Now they were both going to die.

She envisioned the whole thing playing out in her head. Zoe lying on the ground bleeding from a bullet wound, in agony, terrified, having no idea why Amanda had done this to her. Then the glorious moment of triumph when her HRT lover found her, his grief-stricken expression vanishing the instant another bullet took him out, never realizing that he was their real target the entire time.

The thought made her smile.

Chapter Three

Zoe slid behind the wheel of her car, locked the doors then laid her forehead against the steering wheel and closed her eyes. She'd already been feeling like shit when she'd come here but now she was literally sick to her stomach.

What the hell was she going to do?

Swallowing back tears, she raised her head and started the ignition. Clay had wanted to come with her to the appointment but he'd been called in to work for some kind of meeting first thing this morning and she definitely wasn't telling him this over the phone.

The drive home from her doctor's office took almost an hour with the heavy traffic but she barely noticed, in a daze the entire time. When she pulled into the secure underground parking lot, she immediately spotted Clay's truck in its spot and parked next to it. Her mind was a chaotic whirlwind of fear and anxiety.

Upstairs her hand shook as she took out her key to unlock the front door, her stomach a giant knot of nerves. She had a feeling Clay was going to freak out. Hell, *she* was already freaking out and she hated it. She was always in control. She prided herself on it.

When she opened the door, she got another shock to find Celida and Tuck sitting on the living room couch. Her best friend had made it back sooner than they'd expected. Zoe stood there in the entryway, feeling hollowed out, barely able to summon a smile. She couldn't handle company right now, not even her cousin and best friend.

Clay got up and walked toward her. "Hey, how'd it go? Everything okay?"

She put on a smile she was sure didn't reach her eyes and forced a nod. "Yeah."

"Good." His big arms came around her in a gentle hug and she almost lost it. She wanted so badly to cling to him, bury her face against his wide chest and cry. And she wasn't a crier. The guilt from lying just now was gnawing at her. "You still look a bit pale," he said, frowning as he eased back to study her, that intense blue gaze roving over her face. She'd fixed her eye makeup down in the car so he couldn't tell she'd been teary earlier.

"Just tired," she answered, and moved past him to greet the others. She could fake it for a little while until they left. They might be family, but she needed to tell Clay this in private, without anyone else around. "Hey, y'all. I hear there's gonna be a wedding this weekend."

Celida made a guilty face as she got up to hug her, but then a smile replaced it, stretching the scar on her right cheek. Her gray eyes glowed with happiness. "Yeah. Sorry I didn't call you but things were crazy out west."

"It's okay." She released Celida and aimed a smile at her cousin. "So, when and where?"

"We're still working out all the details," Tuck said, and pulled out his phone to show her everything he'd organized already. Zoe responded in all the appropriate places even though she could barely concentrate, tried to seem enthusiastic when all she wanted was for them to leave so she could talk to Clay. God, what the hell was he going to say to her?

"We're slammed at work wrapping up an investigation," Celida told her, flipping the end of her long, chocolate-brown ponytail over one shoulder, "and actually I'm supposed to be at the office right now. I know you've been sick and you've probably got another deadline coming up with your next book, but I'm really stuck. I hate to ask, but could you carve out a few hours to run some errands for us this week?"

Even though she felt completely overwhelmed by the drastic turn her life had just taken two hours ago, she didn't want them to know anything was wrong and there was no way she could say no. "Sure, no problem."

Celida's face brightened. "You're the awesomest friend ever." She hugged Zoe again, sat back on the couch and pulled out her phone.

Tuck shook his head at Zoe and rolled his eyes as Celida took over and efficiently laid out everything she wanted done. "We'll need to try on our dresses right away, see if we need them altered or whatever. And then we'll have to figure out how many people are actually coming so we can get the caterer arranged, but there shouldn't be more than a dozen total. I'm giving you free reign to pick whatever you want for the menu, because I don't really care."

The thought of food at the moment made Zoe want to throw up, but she nodded and dutifully jotted down a list of what Celida needed. A sort of numbness was setting in now, offset by sharp stabs of panic every few minutes as reality intruded again.

"Hey, and Clay told us about the latest message you got from that stalker this morning," Celida finished when they'd gone over everything. "That shit's gotta stop, because it's escalating. I've updated my analyst and she's gonna check it out ASAP."

"Thanks." He was probably just some lonely, social reject trying to get a reaction out of her. Although this latest message had made the blood drain from her face when she'd read it. Which was no doubt his intention, the sick bastard. Just one more thing for her to worry about.

"I sent everything to Rycroft first thing this morning. He's got someone on it now, just in case," Clay said. "She won't be going out alone anymore until we get to the bottom of this," he added with a pointed look at her, aware of how much she hated being a prisoner in her own home because of some jackass, "but if it's at all related to what happened in New Orleans, his people will find out and let us know."

Zoe covered a shiver at the mention of it and crossed her arms to stem the urge to fidget with her hands. Only in the last couple of months had she begun to truly heal from the trauma of what had happened there, and now this freaking stalker had come along to dredge all the memories up again.

Celida nodded, then gave her an encouraging smile. "I'm sure he's just a whacko. Doesn't hurt to be cautious though."

"Yeah," Zoe answered, strung so taut inside it felt like she might shatter. *Now please just go. I love you guys, but I need you to leave right now.*

She figured she did a good enough acting job pretending nothing was wrong, because Celida and Tuck stayed to visit for another half hour or so before leaving. But she hadn't fooled everyone, because the moment Clay shut and locked the door behind them, he turned to face her and put his hands on his hips.

"What's wrong?" he demanded.

Her heart sank. She really shouldn't be surprised that he'd known something was up.

She lowered herself onto the couch. Now that the moment had come, how did she even tell him? Her throat tightened.

Expression filled with concern, he walked toward her, stopped a step away. "Zo. What? What did the doctor say?"

Staring up at his handsome, worried face, Zoe felt her insides tremble. Unwanted tears welled up and she decided there was no easy way to tell him except to just get it out there.

She swallowed. "I'm pregnant."

Wait, *what*?

Clay stared at her as the words penetrated, echoing through his brain. And everything inside him seemed to stop. Even his heart.

Especially his heart.

"Pregnant?" He knew he sounded like a fucking moron, like he didn't know what the word meant, but denial was a bitch. And he was definitely in denial.

Zoe nodded, looking completely miserable, her black-rimmed amber eyes bright with tears. She sniffed, the little diamond stud at the side of her nose catching the light coming in from the window behind her. "Yes. A little over six weeks."

He raked a hand through his hair. "Well what... I mean, how..." Well, he knew *how*, but—*how*? She'd been on the pill, had been from the time they'd moved in together. She took it every day religiously, although maybe not at the same time every day.

This wasn't supposed to happen. Didn't fit the mental plan he'd had in place. Before they even thought about having kids, he'd always assumed they'd be married for a while first. Enjoy life together, just the two of them. And he'd been slowly warming up to *that* idea over the past year. To have this dropped on them was...a shock, to say the least.

She lifted a shoulder, seemed to curl in on herself,

the ends of her pigtails, one red and one black, brushing the tops of her shoulders. "I don't know. The doctor said it sometimes happens, even when a woman is on the pill. I guess we're in the three percent it doesn't always work for," she finished in a small voice.

"And the doc, he's sure?"

A nod. "Blood test and urine test both came back positive. This is real."

Okay, but...holy fuck. A *baby*. He was going to be a father.

A flare of panic burst inside him and he mentally smothered it. He couldn't move, couldn't answer, just stood there staring while his heart slammed against his sternum as though he'd just been trapped alone behind enemy lines.

He wasn't ready for this. Didn't know if he'd *ever* be ready for this. They'd talked about maybe having kids one day, but in a casual, way off in the misty future kind of way.

The thick silence in the room finally registered and then it dawned on him that Zoe looked every bit as freaked out as he felt. "Are you... How do you feel about it?" he managed past the sudden restriction in his throat.

"I'm terrified," she burst out, seeming on the edge of losing it, which freaked him even more, because Zoe rarely cried. "I didn't plan on this. We've only been together a year and I know we're not ready for this. I don't even know what to think because I haven't had time to process it."

He nodded, right there with her, reeling at the reality of this bombshell.

She started to cry then, silently, wiping the tears away before they could fall, and the sight pierced him. He sat next to her and drew her into his arms. "Hey, don't," he began, but she shook her head and cried harder. Wordlessly he held her, not knowing what else to say.

A baby, he thought again in shock. Shit, what the hell did he know about babies? About being a dad? He didn't even like most people, and he had a well-earned reputation of being a hardass.

No, he was rough, gruff, and he knew more about killing than he did about loving someone. Except where Zoe was concerned, but she was a grown woman, not a helpless infant. God. How was he supposed to raise a kid into a normal, functional human being with that kind of resume?

His careening thoughts shifted to his own sister, a strung-out junkie who'd wound up on the streets because of her drug addiction, willing to do whatever—or whomever—to get her next fix. His parents had repeatedly sent her to rehab, to no avail. Finally they'd resorted to taking her home and giving her a daily dose of meth just to keep her close by so they could monitor her. It infuriated and sickened him that they enabled her habit, but now his mother's words to him hit home with the force of a roundhouse to the solar plexus.

You'll never understand what lengths you'll go to for your child until you become a parent yourself.

Well, he was going to find out firsthand in another few months, wasn't he?

At that realization, the panic he'd been holding at bay so far suddenly grabbed him by the throat, squeezed until he could barely swallow. He needed to move, wanted to get up and leave until he got himself together but knew it would shatter Zoe if he left right now. She'd take it as evidence that he didn't want the baby. He didn't *not* want the baby, but he was still struggling to come to grips with everything.

So he stayed put, refusing to move, and just held her close. His doubts and insecurities were his issues, his demons to battle. He wouldn't add to the burden Zoe already carried and say them out loud. God, he'd never seen her like this.

Her shoulders shuddered with the force of her muted sobs, and it sliced him up, made him feel even shittier about the way he'd reacted. Even in the aftermath of what she'd endured at the hands of her kidnapper, she'd never fallen apart like this.

It made him frantic to make it better, only this time, he couldn't. There was no one's ass he could kick, no target to hunt down on her behalf. He cradled the back of her head with one hand and kept his other arm wrapped securely around her ribs, murmured soothing sounds to her.

Shit. He mentally cursed himself for being so freaking clueless when it came to comforting her. He'd just been so stunned and well, dismayed, and now he regretted not being able to hide his reaction better. He felt like he'd let her down in the worst way.

The sound of her crying and trying not to broke his heart. Now he understood why she'd been feeling so tired and not herself recently. Damn, he hated to see her so upset.

Say something, dumbass.

"Hey," he said softly, stroking her back with one hand while he cradled her head to him. "Hey, shhh. It's gonna be okay. It'll be okay." He was mentally shitting his pants right now but he'd be damned if he'd let it show. She was freaked enough as it was, couldn't be good for her or the baby.

She shook her head, sucked in a shaky breath in between hitching breaths, and he held her closer.

He felt frantic with the need to comfort her. *Do something! Make it better!*

"Zo. Come on, we're fine. We're *fine*," he emphasized, speaking next to her ear.

At that she stilled, struggled to get herself back under control. Her whole body jerked as she fought back more tears.

Clay rubbed her back some more, waited for her to calm, catch her breath. And when she finally raised her head to stare up at him through swollen, eyeliner and mascara-smeared eyes, the vise that had been clamped around his chest and gut suddenly eased.

She searched his eyes, worry etched into every line of her face. "What are we going to do? I feel like it's my fault, like maybe I screwed up with my pills or—"

"No." He wiped gently at the black smears beneath her eyes. God, he loved her. Would do anything for her. "I'm as much at fault as you are." Wait. That sounded awful, even to him. Dammit…

He shook his head, frustrated that the right words weren't there, the need to reassure her clawing at him. Part of him wanted to shut the hell up before he made this worse, but he knew he had to say something positive and encouraging.

"What I mean is, I love you and I'm not going anywhere. It's an…adjustment for us both, but look what we've already been through together. This isn't nearly as tough as all that, right?" Logically speaking, anyway.

"Yeah," she answered shakily.

"Yeah," he confirmed. But oh my God, a *father*. To a helpless, innocent baby. He'd never held one but babies were so tiny. What if he did something wrong and freaking broke it?

Or—Mother of Christ, what would he do if it was a *girl*?

He schooled his features into a calm expression, refused to let Zoe see how much he was rattled, especially by that last part. But even he knew he was failing that mission big time.

Her rock. You gotta be her rock, dickhead.

He could lose his shit later on when he was alone.

Man up, sailor.

He was saved from saying something that would likely make things worse by a knock at the door. Zoe stiffened and wiped her face as Clay jumped up and headed over to answer it. Through the peephole he saw Tuck standing out in the hallway.

Stifling a sigh, he opened the door. "Hey. What's up?"

"I texted you but you didn't answer." Tuck's gaze shifted from him to Zoe, and a slight frown creased his brow as he looked at his cousin. "Is uh…everything okay?" he asked her.

"Fine," Zoe said with a forced smile that made Clay's agitation worse, though there was no way Tuck could miss that she'd been crying.

Tuck looked back at him. "Ah, sorry to interrupt, but DeLuca just called. The director's requested a meeting with us all at headquarters."

Now? Clay expelled a sigh, resisted the urge to run a hand through his hair. The timing couldn't be worse. "How long do we have?"

"Thirty minutes."

Shit. Barely enough time to get over there. But what was he going to say, no? "Fine."

"I told Celida I'd catch a ride with you, so she took my truck home."

He grunted in reply, annoyed as hell with this situation. "Gimme a minute." Leaving Tuck in the doorway, he went into the bedroom to grab his wallet, keys and phone.

When he turned around Zoe was standing inside the doorway, hands cupping her elbows as she folded her arms across her middle. Her expression was uncertain, the worry in her gaze tearing at him. He hated leaving her without resolving things, but he had to go.

"I'm sorry about this," he said, crossing the room to pull her into a hug.

She leaned into him, put her arms around his waist, but he could feel the tension in her, the uncertainty. "It's okay," she murmured in a flat tone. "Call me when you're done?"

He pulled away, nodded. "I'll come home right after." Even he knew they had to talk more about this.

"Okay." Her eyes searched his, full of apprehension and something else he couldn't define. She was definitely holding something else back, he knew it. And it was making him nuts that he had to wait to find out what it was.

He put on an encouraging smile. "It'll be okay, raven. Love you."

"Love you too."

Frustrated and feeling more than a little helpless, he kissed her lightly on the mouth and left.

Chapter Four

As luck would have it, Zoe did show up at the coffee shop the next morning.

Except she wasn't alone.

Amanda ducked down lower in the driver's seat of her rental minivan, her pulse picking up as the two women entered through the front door. She'd finally found her.

The large sunglasses concealed Amanda's eyes and the hat covered her hair, which she'd shoved beneath it. Not that she was worried about Zoe recognizing her—they'd never met before, although Amanda knew all about her. But this place would have security cameras and she didn't want any intelligence agencies being able to trace her once this job was done. The FBI and probably NSA had to be tracking her now, or at least trying to. She had to be extra careful not to get caught.

Using a pair of binoculars she made sure no one was looking her way, then held them to her eyes and studied her target through the large windows along the rear of the coffee shop. The two women were chatting, their backs to Amanda. Zoe's friend was slightly shorter, with an hourglass figure. And she dressed like a normal human being instead of like some sideshow freak.

No surprise, Zoe was in full Goth mode again today. Black, ruffled Victorian-style skirt showing beneath the hem of her equally weird jacket. Today it appeared her hair was dyed red on the right side of her head and black on the other, and she had her trademark heavy black eye makeup and bright red lip thing going as per usual. Ridiculous.

But then the other woman with her turned around, and Amanda's heart sunk. She knew that face. The scar on her right cheek was a dead giveaway.

Special Agent Celida Morales. Former Marine, now in the domestic terrorism division of the FBI.

But she was also the fiancée of Brad Tucker, one of the HRT's team leaders.

Amanda lowered the binoculars, the wheels in her head turning. As she reached for her cell phone, the dread faded and an idea took shape. This wasn't what she'd originally planned, but there might be an opportunity here.

She dialed Dominic, waited impatiently for the call to go through. He picked up on the second ring. "I've got her," she said without preamble. "I'm at a coffee shop about twenty minutes from Quantico. But she's with a female FBI agent—who just happens to be engaged to another HRT member."

"What about the guys, are any of them around?"

"No. How soon can you get here?" This could be perfect.

He gave an annoyed sigh. "Do you even know if the team is in town?"

Did he think she was a total idiot? "Yes. They were in Alaska until a couple days ago and my contact said they're back in town."

"You trust him?"

"No reason not to." After fucking him on and off for the past week she'd promised to pay him a small amount of the reward if he came through for her with decent intel. A fair trade, as far as she was concerned.

"I still don't know about targeting one of the females to get to the team. That's not gonna get us the money. And it might just get us captured or killed. "

Not any female. *Zoe*. "It's the only way to find them," she insisted, stubbornly sticking to her plan. Zoe had to be part of the setup.

A pause. "I can be there in about thirty minutes."

Her eyes widened. "What? Are you insane? They won't be here in thirty minutes. Where the hell are you?"

"Hang on." There was a sleepy female murmur in the background.

Amanda set her jaw. "We're on the brink of doing this job, and you're busy getting laid?"

"My personal life is none of your business," he shot back. "I was out all night doing recon, and I'm going back out shortly. Look, just follow one of them then, and see where they go. I'm heading out now. If one of them goes home, we'll have a location to stake out. I'll be able to meet you where they stop next."

She didn't have much choice at the moment. "Fine. But get rid of whoever that is and wait for my call. This could be our lucky day." This time she hung up on him before he could answer.

The minutes seemed to crawl by as she waited for Zoe and Celida to come out of the shop. Her plan had been to take Zoe alone, but...

She thought of the pistol tucked into the glove compartment, briefly considered trying to get a shot off now. No. Too risky. It was broad daylight, there were too many people around, and Celida was well trained. Far better trained with a weapon than Amanda, and there was no doubt the female agent would be armed.

No. She should wait. Stick to the original plan, lock down an address so Dominic could come and take care of business while she stood watch, ready to grab her prey.

Tamping down her impatience, Amanda waited while the women climbed into a silver sedan and pulled out of the parking lot. She waited a few seconds, let two cars get between them, then followed.

But they didn't drive to any residential neighborhoods, they drove downtown instead, to a busy shopping district. Twice Amanda nearly lost them in heavy traffic, cursed as she jerked the wheel to avoid being T-boned by a pickup when she ran a red light to catch up.

Her heart beat too fast, impatience making her reckless. She had to chill, get a grip. Celida would be trained in surveillance. If Amanda ran any more lights or made it obvious she was following them, Celida would notice. She wished she'd been able to get a tracking device on the car, but it had been too chancy.

She pulled back, maintained a safe distance from the silver car. It parked along the curb in front of a row of shops and the women went inside. As Amanda passed by she studied the shop.

A caterer. The windows were covered by blinds, so she couldn't see inside. And there was no damn parking on this entire freaking block, she thought in annoyance.

There was nowhere to go but forward.

She circled the block a few times, never able to find a place to park. By the time she came around the fourth time, the silver car had pulled out into traffic and was driving through the next intersection. Amanda shot a glance to her left, saw an opening and veered around the car in front of her.

Horns blared, several vehicles coming at her slammed on their brakes, but she didn't stop. She sped through the intersection, determined not to lose that silver car.

But two lights later she was stuck at a red and the car slipped out of sight.

Cursing, she picked up her phone and dialed her male contact. She'd vowed not to be anyone's whore again, but one last lay or a blowjob would be worth it if it helped her nail Zoe. "I need you to trace a plate for me, right now."

Zoe might have just bought herself some more time, but it wouldn't change anything in the end. She was still going to die.

****

Reclining on the red Victorian velvet living room sofa she'd hauled here from New Orleans, Zoe finally decided to concede defeat and put her laptop on the black-lacquered coffee table beside her. She'd been sitting here for nearly three hours and hadn't gotten a damn word down in her manuscript. Usually the last few chapters of a book flowed easily for her, but not this time.

After all the hours she'd put into researching and writing the draft, a satisfying way to end this book continued to elude her. There were too many loose threads to tie up, too many things still unresolved between her hero and heroine.

Much like they were between her and Clay.

Things weren't…going so well with them. His meeting yesterday had turned into a series of meetings that hadn't ended until almost ten. By the time he'd rolled in the door she'd been in bed fast asleep and she'd been too exhausted to talk when he'd slid in beside her.

She'd slept like a dead woman until he'd rolled out of bed at five this morning to hit the range with the guys, and he'd been gone all day. Part of her wondered if he was avoiding another conversation about the baby because he didn't know what to say, but the longer it took for them to talk, the more her worry increased.

Honestly she didn't know how much more stress she could handle right now. The deadline for this book was Monday morning, but she didn't even care right now because she couldn't concentrate.

There was a baby growing inside her.

It was all she'd been able to think about since finding out the news yesterday. Even when she and Celida had been out running a couple quick errands this morning, she'd barely been able to pay attention to what her best friend had said. Zoe had wanted to tell her so badly, and couldn't, because she and Clay hadn't talked about telling anyone else yet.

He'd seemed as stunned as she'd felt when she'd told him the news yesterday, and even though he hadn't freaked out she worried he was putting on a brave face for her and not telling her how he really felt. Clay was a master of hiding his emotions. As a result she felt restless, unsettled, which was totally unlike her. But little wonder.

Things had been so wonderful between them up to now, and Zoe couldn't help but worry that this might damage their relationship permanently. She didn't blame him for not being excited about the baby when she herself was still trying to come to grips with this.

Her emotions had been in chaos since yesterday morning. At the moment she was ten percent excited and ninety percent scared about becoming a mother, only because this had happened without being planned.

And yet…she was already emotionally attached to the life growing inside her. She'd always been a natural caregiver and felt protective of the baby now, even though she was still trying to adapt to her new role as a mother in a few more months.

She chewed her bottom lip. Clay had said everything would be okay, but what if he felt trapped later on because the decision to become a father had been made for him?

She didn't *think* he would, but if it turned out she was wrong, then he wasn't the man she'd thought he was, and not the man she wanted to spend the rest of her life with.

Nerves buzzed in her stomach until she couldn't stand it anymore. Pushing up, she walked into the kitchen to grab her cell phone and dialed Clay, but it went straight to voicemail. His silence, whether intentional or not, made her heart heavy.

Walking back into the living room, she stood there staring at the blood-red feature wall she'd painted, lined with shelves displaying her collection of bats and skulls and ravens. She'd been teased and bullied because of her Goth style since she was a teenager. Turned out her ex-husband had hated it too. But not Clay.

From day one he'd accepted her as she was. He had hung these shelves for her, had obediently moved all the heavy antique furniture around the condo without complaint until she was satisfied with the layout of each room. Even after moving in here, he'd never tried to change things. Never tried to change *her*.

She might be a strong, confident woman who didn't give a shit what most people thought of her, but she cared what Clay thought. And she loved him to death for allowing her the room to be herself. God, things had to work out between them. *Had* to.

Sinking back onto the sofa, out of desperation she called Celida.

Her friend picked up almost immediately. "Hey, Zozo."

Damn, it felt good just to hear her voice, Celida's steadiness palpable even through the phone line. "Hi. Am I interrupting anything important?"

"Not really, and I can make myself available if you need me. Is this about the cake? Because like I told you, I don't even care what kind you decide on."

"You'd care if it was a red velvet Dracula cake that

looked like it was bleeding when you slice it open in front of your guests." Personally Zoe found the idea awesome.

"Would not. We're just gonna eat it all anyway. So, what's up?" When Zoe hesitated, Celida spoke again. "Hey. You okay?"

She blew out a breath, rubbed her fingertips over her forehead. "I need a private best friend convo."

"Oh, wow. Okay, hang on a sec." She must have put the phone to her chest or something because her voice was muffled as she spoke to whoever was in the room with her and then Zoe heard a door close. "All right, it's just me. So what's up? What did Bauer do now?"

The mention of his name made her throat tighten. Pregnancy hormones already? Or was she just losing her mind? "He didn't do anything. Well, he did, but not on purpose."

Celida was silent a moment. "What did he do, Zo?"

"We both did it." More than a few times at the exact wrong time in her cycle, as it turned out. "I'm pregnant," she blurted.

Celida's shocked silence said it all.

"You can't tell anyone," Zoe rushed on. "Swear you won't say anything, not even to Tuck."

"I can't keep a secret like that from him!"

"You have to! Clay and I have barely even talked about the whole thing because he got called away yesterday in the middle of it, so I probably shouldn't be telling you, but I can't stand not being able to talk to someone about this."

"Okay, so this is…unexpected, I gather? I mean, you don't sound overly thrilled about it and you never mentioned to me about wanting to have a baby."

"It was an accident." Wait, she had to stop saying that. She refused to think about this baby as being an *accident*. It wasn't fair to the child and never wanted her son or daughter to think he or she wasn't wanted. "I mean, no, we didn't plan for this to happen." But it was, and if Clay decided he wasn't ready to be a father then she'd have no choice but to leave him. The very thought made her want to cry.

"Well that's…wow."

The sinking feeling in her stomach was becoming way too familiar. "Yeah. I know."

"So when did you tell him?"

"Right after you guys left yesterday."

"I knew something was up! I said to Tuck as we were walking to the elevator that I thought something was up. I can't believe you didn't say anything to me yesterday, or this morning when we were alone. So how'd he take it?"

"He was shocked, same as I was, but he didn't freak out. Said it would be okay, cuddled me while I lost it." He hadn't freaked, hadn't accused her of getting pregnant behind his back. Those were positive signs, right?

"Wow. That's impressive, especially for Bauer."

Zoe huffed out a laugh. "He's come a long way since we've been together. And now I can't stop worrying that this is going to ruin everything between us." If it did, however, she was gone.

Celida snorted. "Okay, you must not have been sleeping enough lately because that's just crazy talk. That man might be rough around the edges, but he's crazy about you."

Zoe nibbled on a black-painted fingernail, all her subconscious fears bubbling to the surface. "Yeah, but what if he feels trapped or something once the baby's born? Being a dad. You know how commitment-phobic he was when he and I got together. I don't want him sticking around out of a sense of duty." That's why she was feeling so freaking insecure about this whole thing.

"He won't." Celida sounded absolutely certain on that. "But Zo, come on, just phone the man. You need to be talking to him about this right now, not me."

"I know." She slumped into the corner of the sofa, dragged her favorite bat-and-jack 'o lantern-lap quilt over her legs. "I haven't been able to get hold of him."

"Hmm, Tuck did mention he'd be busy today, so I guess the whole team is involved in whatever's going on."

Zoe sighed. "It's just not how I'd planned it all out in my head. I thought eventually he'd get over his phobia about marriage and then pop the question. We'd get married soon after that and then have a few years together as a married couple at least before we even thought about having kids."

"I get that. And jeez, speaking of marriage, we'd better get our dresses sized right away because I'm betting your boobs are already bigger than they were a couple weeks ago."

Zoe smiled a little at Celida's teasing tone. "Well if they're going to be this sore, they damn well better at least give me another cup size." She'd always been smaller on top than on the bottom, a true pear shape. Might be kinda nice to have more up top for a change. And come to think of it, her bras were pretty snug now.

Celida laughed. "So, when's the big day? Spring? And how are you feeling? Sick at all?"

"Middle of May, and I feel fine, except my boobs are unbelievably sore and I sometimes feel like I'm a little hung over, especially in the mornings."

"May's the perfect time to have a baby."

"Says the woman who's not pregnant." But already the anxiety she'd been fighting with all day was fading. She should have just told Celida first thing when her friend had picked her up this morning, on the way to the coffee shop. She would have felt so much better about all this. "Mostly I just hate that it's happened this way."

Celida snorted. "Well it did. He's a grown man, Zo, and he was just as responsible for the making of this baby as you were. He can suck it up, like you have."

Leave it to Celida to get right to the heart of it. "I know, and he will. But…" She paused before continuing. "I really wanted to be married before I became a mother." She'd never told Celida that before, but it was important to her.

"You can still get married before the baby comes."

She shook her head. "No way. I'm not telling him we need to get married, the day after telling him we're having an unplanned baby." Zoe had been through a divorce too, but it had been much more amicable than Clay's. The last thing she wanted to do was pressure him into marrying her simply because it was what she wanted.

"Hon, does he even know you want to get married?"

"He knows I want to get married *someday*, but I think that timeline is shorter for me than for him. I've been careful not to bring it up much, but we've talked about it a few times since we've been together. In passing, you know. Making plans for down the road."

A pause. "I can't believe you of all people are walking on eggshells around the man you want to spend the rest of your life with!" She sounded exasperated.

Zoe winced. "God, I know," she murmured, disgusted with herself. "I don't know what's wrong with me. Seriously." Where the hell was all this insecurity coming from? She prided herself on always speaking her mind, not taking any shit from anyone, and Clay knew very well just how blunt she could be. With this one topic as an exception, apparently.

"I don't want him to propose just because I'm pregnant," she continued. "I want him to want me for *me*. And you know how it is with the FBI significant others outside of our inner circle. They're nice and all, but the married ones won't fully accept me until we make it legal. Until then, I'm an outsider." Not because the Bureau wives were being bitchy. It's just how things were in the law enforcement world.

"I know, and that sucks. The legal reasons are one of the main reasons why Tuck and I decided not to wait any longer."

Zoe could understand why. Their job as part of the HRT was dangerous, and life was unpredictable. "It's not just legal reasons for me though. We've been together long enough that he should know whether he wants to marry me or not." Dammit, now she was starting to get mad.

"Then tell him how you feel." Celida huffed out a chuckle. "And I can safely say that is something I literally *never* thought I would have to say to you."

"Yeah, I'll bet," she said with a half-smile. "I guess I'm just…scared it won't turn out the way I want it to." That kind of rejection after everything they'd built together, and the prospect of raising their child alone, would gut her. "God, maybe my divorce messed me up after all."

Celida made a sympathetic sound. "You gotta tell him the truth, Zo."

"How do I do that without making it seem like I'm pressuring him?" To be honest it had bothered her for a while now that he didn't seem to want to take the next step in their relationship. She knew he trusted her, so it had to be his own baggage holding him back. She'd been patient with him up 'til now, but with a baby on the way she wasn't sure how much longer she could stay silent about it.

And, if marriage wasn't an option for him, then she'd have to leave at some point before the baby came. The thought made her heart clench because he was her whole world and getting married due to an ultimatum wasn't what she wanted.

"Hon, call your man," Celida ordered. "*Talk* to him. He needs to know all this. And if he doesn't answer, call

Tuck. Or DeLuca. They'll track him down."

Zoe smiled at that. "Yeah, sure." She let out a sigh. "Thanks, *bébé*. I appreciate it. And I feel way better now." She placed her hand on her belly, smiled at the thought of the life protected inside her body. "I'm gonna be a mama, Lida."

"I know, and it's so surreal. But damn, I don't know how I'm going to keep Tuck in the dark about this."

"Ha, yeah you do. Tight-lipped control freak." She said it with affection.

"Yeah, okay, guilty on all counts. Look, I gotta run, but call me tonight if you want to talk again. I'm here for you and the baby, no matter what."

Celida's protectiveness and loyalty made her smile wider. "I know. Love you."

"Love you too."

Zoe set the phone down for a moment, feeling relieved now that she'd gotten everything off her chest. She glanced at the clock. Almost seven.

Quit stalling and call him already, she scolded herself.

Bracing herself just in case, Zoe dialed Clay.

Chapter Five

Clay eased the condo door open, a little disappointed to find the lights off in the kitchen and living room. He'd called Zoe back as he was leaving the base just under half an hour ago. It was almost eleven but she'd said she'd wait up because they needed to talk.

Normally he considered those words to be the most dangerous in the English language for a man, but he needed to talk to her too. She'd been so upset earlier, and upon reflection, his reaction to the news had sucked big time.

A band of gold light was coming from beneath their closed master bedroom door. He pushed that open, found Zoe sitting up reading in their king-size antique four-poster bed, her back resting against the heavy carvings of the dark walnut headboard.

She set her book aside, pulled the black-and-white skull print comforter up higher on her body and gave him an uncertain smile. "Hi."

"Hi." He closed the door, suddenly didn't know what to say. "Sorry I couldn't get home sooner. Things have been crazy." They'd met with the top FBI officials for most of the day, going over the op in Alaska.

"It's fine." A beat of taut silence followed.

Unwilling to let this go on any longer, Clay crossed the room and sank onto the edge of the bed next to her, his hip touching the outline of her thigh through the blankets. He reached for her hand, twined their fingers together, the worst of the tension in his chest easing at the contact. "So how are you feeling?"

"A little better." She searched his eyes, her tentativeness so unlike her. "You?"

"Good." He looked down at her still-flat abdomen, covered by the blankets, then back up at her face. "Pretty unreal still, huh?"

"Yes." She shifted, broke eye contact, and he knew something was off.

He squeezed her hand, hating the sense of dread coiling inside him. Why wouldn't she tell him what was wrong? She was holding back something big, he knew it, and didn't like it. "Tell me what's wrong."

She blew out a breath, met his gaze once more. "I'm worried about us."

He blinked at that, taken aback. She was pretty blunt when she had something to say, but this caught him totally off guard. "What? Why?" He hurriedly tried to think of what he might have done recently to make her feel insecure about their relationship, but came up blank.

She made an exasperated sound. "Because we didn't plan for this and I know you're worried and trying not to show it. Plus I'm scared you don't believe me that it was an accident—"

What the hell? *That's* what she'd been worrying about? He opened his mouth to shoot that one down but she just kept talking, not giving him a chance to respond.

"I'm afraid you're going to blame me for this, that you'll resent me and the baby, wake up one day down the road and accuse me of trapping you and ruining your life and—"

"Whoa, stop. *No.*" He pulled her into his arms and hugged her close, one hand cradling the back of her head. Jesus, he'd had no idea she'd been thinking those things. Where the hell had all that come from? "Why would you ever think that?" Her reaction was a kick in the gut and the last thing he'd expected. It felt like she'd sucker punched him in the solar plexus.

"I don't know," she shot back, but clearly she did know, otherwise she wouldn't have thought it in the first place. Dammit, it freaking hurt that she'd think so little of him.

Zoe leaned against him and drew in a shaky breath, her arms tucked up against his chest.

Holding her to his chest, Clay lowered his head to speak close to her ear and fought back the sudden spike in his temper. Getting mad at her would only push her away and that was the last thing he wanted. "I would never think any of those things. I know I can be an asshole sometimes, but Jesus." If she seriously thought he was like that, why the hell was she even with him?

No. Breathe.

Had to be the shock of it all, he reasoned with himself. She was overwhelmed, wasn't thinking straight. But dammit, those comments had smarted. Didn't she trust him more than that? They'd been through so much together in the last year and he'd grown a lot, had put a lot of effort into letting his past go and moving forward with her. Why would she ever think he'd blame her for something like this when it was clearly both their doing?

Zoe didn't answer, now curled into him, and his initial burst of anger faded when he realized she was tensed up, as if she expected him to blast her.

Clay sighed and forced his muscles to relax. Hard as that had been to hear, he was just glad she'd finally said it. He couldn't believe she'd been carrying that around for the past day and a half, on top of the shock of finding out she was pregnant. No freaking wonder she'd been so upset yesterday.

More defensive denials rose up but he bit them back, ordered himself to calm the hell down. This wasn't about him right now, it was about her. He knew she was scared. She needed him to be her rock right now, reassure her that her fears were unfounded. Not to lose it because she'd doubted him and hurt his ego. "It wasn't anybody's fault, it just happened," he said quietly.

She drew back to look him in the eye. "So you're not mad at me? Tell me the truth."

She *still* didn't believe him? God, she was shredding him.

To make sure he got through to her once and for all, he took her face between his hands, stared down into her golden eyes as he spoke. "I'm not mad at you. We didn't mean for it to happen but it did, and now we're going to have to deal with it."

Shit, that sounded harsh, didn't it?

"I mean, we're in this together," he rephrased, hoping that made up for his brain-dead comment a second ago. "I would never walk out on you, or the baby. Ever. God, Zo, I can't believe you'd ever even worry about that. I love you. I'm not going anywhere." That was better, right? It was so damn hard to think past everything she'd just said.

His efforts were rewarded when hope bloomed in her gaze, followed by a tentative smile playing at the corners of her mouth. "You're sure."

He nodded. "Yes. I know you're scared and that this has been a big surprise to us both, but it's gonna be fine. *We're* gonna be fine." Did that sound sensitive and supportive enough? He hoped so, but hell if he knew anymore.

She wound her arms around his neck and squeezed him hard, so he guessed he'd finally said something right. The tightness in his chest eased. "I love you too. But oh my God, I'm so not ready for this."

Yeah, he knew how that felt. "We'll figure it out. And you're gonna be an amazing mom."

Pulling back a little to look at him, he caught an uncharacteristic flash of insecurity in her eyes. "You think so?"

"I know so." Not a doubt in his mind that their baby had won the mama lottery with Zoe. Hell, the woman had been kidnapped because she'd risked her life to help an abused woman and her child leave that fucker Ruiz back in New Orleans.

She was a natural protector and a nurturer. He'd never met anyone who liked to hug as much as Zoe did. Friend, relative or total stranger, didn't matter. And when Zoe hugged someone, she hugged them like she meant it. Just one of the many reasons she'd succeeded in melting his ice-encrusted heart.

Him? Not so much. Clay could protect, but he sucked at nurturing. Just look at him now, ham-fisting his way through this.

Shoving that unsettling thought aside, he cleared his throat and released her. "Feel better now?"

She let out a sigh full of relief. "Yes." She put a hand to his cheek, stared into his eyes. "I'm sorry for doubting you. It's just that, given what happened with Eve... You told me how she always lied and manipulated to get her way, and that you were cynical about women in general until we got together. I was worried that this might trigger all that again, that you wouldn't trust me now."

Okay, he guessed that made a tiny bit of sense from that perspective. Kind of. After his reality-show-worthy divorce it was no secret that he'd been bitter and cynical about a *lot* of things. Still… "I'm not the same person I was back then." Being with Zoe had changed him. For the better.

She inclined her head. "I know that," she said, looking guilty. "I do."

He exhaled a hard breath. "I guess I just assumed that after all this time and everything we've been through together, you'd *know* I trust you completely. More than I trust anyone else." Even his teammates, guys he trusted with his life on and off the job, so that said a lot. It stung like a bitch to find out that she obviously didn't trust him to that same extent.

Her answering smile took some of the lingering hurt away. "I'm glad you do. And I still feel awful for thinking what I did. I'm sorry."

He believed her. He nodded once, even though he was still smarting inside, and in that moment realized just how far he'd come over the past year. The old Clay would have held onto the hurt, would have let the resentment build into a toxic mass inside him until it eventually shot out of his mouth at her in a gush of nasty words intended to inflict maximum pain.

The new Clay understood what a dick move that tactic was, that he had to be a grown up and let it go instead. She'd apologized, he'd accepted; now they had to move forward.

But it wasn't easy. Some part of him still wanted to lash out at her for hurting him. He fought it back, refused to go there. Zoe didn't deserve that.

"So you said six weeks," he said to change the subject. "That gives us how long until…" He was going to say D-Day, but managed to stop himself before the insensitive words came out. And if they were having a baby, then he really needed to clean up his mouth over the next few months, or the kid's first words would be choice ones.

Her expression brightened. She tucked a lock of black hair behind her left ear, the long red strands on the right curling over her shoulder. "Due date is May seventeenth."

His eyes widened a little at that. Holy hell. Having an actual date for it made this way too real.

"Oh. Okay." He was quiet a moment, letting that sink in. "So what did the doctor say? Do we need to be doing anything different?" Because he distinctly remembered how he'd shoved her down on the mattress last night and pinned her beneath him while he'd fucked her from behind, and none too gently at the end.

She let out a husky chuckle. "No, everything's fine. I'm not going to break or anything. I'll need to start taking prenatal vitamins and watching my diet a little better than I have been though. I'll get regular checkups from now on but I'm not considered high risk or anything so everything should be fine." She tried a smile, but it seemed weary, and he couldn't shake that damn nagging feeling that she was still keeping something else from him. It was driving him crazy. "We can still have sex whenever we want."

Thank God, he thought, expelling a relieved breath. Because he'd go insane if he couldn't connect with her that way for the next few months. Their sex life was amazing, and it was the way he felt most comfortable expressing to Zoe how much he loved and wanted her. He was way better with actions than words.

He stroked a hand over her lower back, glad that things seemed all right between them again. "Okay, so how do you want to handle this? You want to tell our parents first?"

She shook her head. "I think I'd rather wait until after the first trimester, just in case. I don't know. I'm still trying to come to grips with this mentally, so I need some time to adjust before we say anything."

"Sure, that makes sense."

She let out a long sigh and groaned. "God, I'm wiped. I need a bath."

"Yeah, go ahead." Whatever she needed, he would make sure she got it. "Want me to draw it for you?"

One side of her mouth quirked up and her eyes sparkled with humor. "I'm not an invalid, but thanks. I'll take a rain check on that though. Because in a few more months I'll be so big I'm probably going to need help getting in and out of the tub," she finished, her voice wry.

Clay had a sudden flash of her standing before him with a very swollen belly and he did another mental freak out, even while the most primitive part of him was in full protective mode. His woman needed him, and he wouldn't let her down. His sensitivity chip was smaller than a lot of guys', but at least since Zoe it was functioning again. Man, this still felt surreal though. He'd always thought he'd be the last guy on the team to become a father.

"Yeah." He even managed to put on a comforting smile.

When the bathroom door closed behind her and he was sure she couldn't see him, he leaned forward and dropped his head into his hands with a low groan. It had been a hell of a week so far. Of all the things that could have happened to him right now, this one hadn't even been on his radar. And to find out Zoe still felt insecure about his love and intentions made him feel like shit.

In SEAL training the famous saying went, *"The only easy day was yesterday"*.

Those six words had never rung more true for him than they did right now. As of yesterday morning his entire world had shifted on its axis and there was nothing he could do now but man up and slay his inner demons. Zoe and their baby needed him.

Ready or not, personal baggage about having kids or

not…

In eight months' time, he and Zoe were going to be parents.

****

Zoe emerged from the bathroom a while later, wrapped in her favorite red satin robe, and found Clay fixing himself a sandwich in the kitchen. The overhead lights gleamed on his short, dark hair and outlined the muscular width of his shoulders and upper back that stretched the fabric of his black T-shirt.

He glanced back at her, gave her a small smile but she read him well and could see the tension in his back and shoulders.

She'd hurt him, this proud, strong man, even though she hadn't meant to. Knowing that sliced her up inside.

Stepping up behind him, she slid her arms around his waist and pressed herself to his broad back. His muscles were taut. "I'm sorry I hurt you." When he didn't respond right away she continued. "Do you forgive me?"

He stayed still for a second, then set down the bread and knife and turned to face her. Setting a finger beneath her chin, he tipped her face up and looked into her eyes, the intensity of his gaze making her heart pound. "Yes, I forgive you. Know why? Because I love you. You mean *everything* to me. Everything, Zo, and…dammit, I thought you knew it." He shook his head once, his gaze full of frustration. He ran a hand through his hair. "I swore I'd let it go and not say anything else, but the truth is, I can't stand knowing you'd ever doubt me having your back."

She swallowed around the sudden constriction in her throat. She knew he struggled with expressing his emotions verbally. It made his words a hundred times more powerful.

"You're right," she said softly, "and I shouldn't have needed the reminder. I love you to death, I'll always have your back too, and I would never hurt you for the world."

Needing to kiss him, to soothe and heal the damage she'd done, she lifted up on tiptoe to press her lips to his. A rush of relief hit her when his muscles relaxed and he cupped the back of her head to deepen the kiss. A slow, firm possession.

When he raised his head a moment later, there was no hint of frustration left in his eyes and she knew he'd truly forgiven her. She also vowed never to make the mistake of doubting him again. "Glad that's done with."

His lips twitched. "Me too." That vivid blue gaze delved into hers. "But why do I still get the feeling something else is bothering you that you're not telling me about?"

Surprise flashed through her at his perception. Maybe it was his years of honing his observation skills in the SEAL Teams, or maybe it was because he'd had to be vigilant to protect himself from Eve, but he saw everything, even when she tried to hide it.

"What? No," she lied, unwilling to talk about marriage right now.

Things were too raw between them just yet; she wasn't going to risk pushing him away. And she needed a chance to adjust to being pregnant first. Maybe she was hurt and confused about not knowing his intentions as far as getting married were concerned, but if Clay proposed now she'd never know if it was only because of the baby. Before she had that conversation with him, she needed to emotionally regroup.

Clay gave her a look that said he knew she was lying, but thankfully let it go. "Okay." He released her and went back to making his sandwich, but it felt like a dismissal. "How's the book coming along? Get any work done today?"

"Not really." Maybe now that the worst of her anxiety had been soothed, she could find the words again. "Did you get the bachelor party stuff started?"

He laid the butter knife aside. "Yeah, everything's pretty much done."

"Guess I'd better get cracking on the bridal shower then."

Ensconced on the couch while Clay finished making his dinner, she grabbed her laptop and opened her contacts to send out a group e-mail to the girls. She glanced at the new messages that popped into her inbox, and her blood froze when she saw another message from her stalker, sent from yet another address.

For a second she debated ignoring it but knew it would eat at her until she read the thing.

Taking a steadying breath, she steeled herself and opened it. A picture of an hourglass appeared, most of the sand already in the bottom glass, a thin trickle spilling from the scant amount in the upper bulb.

Time's almost out, Zoe. Are you scared? You should be. I'm coming for you.

She blanched and set a protective hand over her abdomen. *Nobody* was threatening her unborn child. "Clay," she said.

He was at her side in three seconds, taking the laptop from her. When he saw the message his expression turned black. "That motherfucker."

He set the computer down and pulled out his phone, called someone. Within a few moments of the conversation starting, she knew it had to be Rycroft. Clay relayed the message and forwarded it to him. "Got it," he answered a few moments later, then hung up, his gaze full of frustration. "Rycroft's got his people looking at it."

"Good," she sighed.

Clay knelt in front of her, put a hand on her nape, concern in his eyes. "You okay?" he murmured, his touch and worry for her a balm to her rattled nerves.

She nodded. Fuck this shit. "I just want that asshole caught."

"Me too." Clay hugged her tight. The moment his powerful arms closed around her, the residual unease she'd been carrying subsided. He made her feel completely safe, and she wished to God she'd never doubted him the way she had. "I'm here for you. You know that, right?"

"Yes."

Leaning back, he gazed into her eyes, his expression fierce. "I told you once that I'd never let you down again. And I won't. I'm not gonna let anything happen to you."

Zoe bit her lip, her heart squeezing. She loved this man so much it hurt. "I know you won't."

He nodded once in satisfaction. "Good."

Cradling the side of his face with one hand, she pressed a tender kiss to his lips then pulled away and gave him a smile. "It's late, but I'd better text the girls about the shower before I get too distracted."

She got up and strode to the kitchen island to get her cell phone, refusing to let that freaking sick psycho mess with her already over-stressed mind tonight. It was so frustrating, that the FBI and NSA had yet to be able to catch the guy.

Whoever he was, he knew what he was doing, knew how to evade detection. At least thus far.

God, it felt like everything in her life was outside of her control right now, and she hated it. While Clay stood beside her at the island eating his sandwich, she began scrolling through her team contacts. Time to take control of something, no matter how small.

Chapter Six

C lay packed the last of his gear into his locker and let out a jaw-cracking yawn. God, he was wiped. He'd barely slept since finding out about the baby the other day and it was catching up with him fast. Back in his Navy days he'd routinely gone two or three days without sleep, but his body wasn't twenty-five anymore.

"Zoe keeping you up past your bedtime?"

Clay looked over his shoulder at a smirking Schroder, the team's newest member and the best combat medic he'd ever worked with. Since the guy was a former Air Force PJ, that wasn't surprising. "Something like that, yeah."

Schroder grinned and slapped him on the back. "Atta boy. Glad to hear it. Taya's been keeping me up late a lot since we got back too." After waggling his eyebrows he stowed his own gear in a locker four down from Clay's. "So, we still on for tonight?"

"Yep. Nineteen hundred hours out at the farm." One of DeLuca's friends had given them permission to use his sixty acres of farmland for the night for the "bachelor party". Clay had set up the fire pit and taken a couple barbecues out there last night before Zoe had called, put up the targets and barricades for the night-vision paintball game he'd planned. "I've still gotta pick up the food and the beer. You want a ride out there? I'm driving Tuck— promised Zoe and Celida I'd get the groom-to-be there and back safely. Maybe Evers, too."

"Sure, that'd be great." He swung his head around to look at Vance, whose right arm was still wrapped up tight against his chest, his dark skin a stark contrast to the white bandages. Though he was in great shape and the second biggest guy on the team, next to Clay, Vance was only human. And this line of work was hell on their bodies. "You're coming tonight too, right?"

"Yeah, but Carm and I fly out first thing tomorrow so I can't stay that long. I'll catch a ride with Cruzie."

"Okay, I'll pick you up around six," Clay said to Schroder. He grabbed his keys and headed out of the team room into the hallway. DeLuca flagged him down.

"Hey. Got a minute?" his commander asked.

"Yeah, sure." Clay followed him into his office.

DeLuca nodded at the chair opposite his desk, his green gaze sharp. "Have a seat."

Frowning, he lowered himself into the chair, had just opened his mouth to ask what was up when Tuck appeared in the doorway. His buddy shut the door behind him and walked over to sit on the edge of DeLuca's desk, both of them staring at Clay.

"What's going on?" Clay demanded.

DeLuca folded his arms over his chest. "We were wondering the same thing."

"I don't follow."

Tuck gave him a *get real* look. "It's obvious to everybody here that you haven't been yourself the past couple days, since we got back from Alaska. You've been distracted. And antisocial, even for you."

Clay felt himself flush. "It's nothing, don't worry about it." Since he'd cleared the air with Zoe last night he felt way better, although his gut was nagging at him that something was still unresolved. But he wasn't so deep into his head about it that he couldn't concentrate on an op.

"So it's not the Alaska op? It's personal, then?" DeLuca asked.

"Yes." Very. And he didn't feel like talking about it.

"But you're okay?" Tuck pressed.

There'd been a lot to deal with over the past week. The cruise ship op, the online threat to Zoe's security, and now the baby. It was still sinking in, the idea of him being a dad soon. He wasn't scared of it now, more just battling his personal demons about not being a good enough dad.

"Yeah." He understood and even appreciated why Tuck and DeLuca were checking up on him though. It was their job to ensure every guy on the team had his head where it needed to be, not distracted on a mission or in training. Because distracted operators got people killed. "I'm good guys, but thanks."

"Has it got anything to do with the situation with Zoe's stalker?" DeLuca asked.

"That's…part of it," he conceded.

He was angry and increasingly worried about the entire situation, and he felt weird about leaving her alone right now, but that wasn't all of it. It was eating him up inside that she was still keeping something from him, and he wished he could talk to someone other than Zoe about the baby. These were guys he trusted with his life. He knew Zoe had already told Celida last night, so he figured she wouldn't be mad if he told Tuck and DeLuca. But in all honestly he just didn't think they would be able to relate.

"Any word on who it is yet?" Tuck asked.

"No, not yet. She got another message last night that

scared her pretty bad, even though she's fronting like it didn't." His woman was strong, one of the things he admired most about her, but he knew she was rattled. And after almost losing her when she'd been held hostage last September, his protective instincts were on red alert right now, even more this time because she was pregnant.

"I passed it on to Rycroft," he continued. "He's bumped it up in terms of priority, said he'd let me know personally once they have anything. Whoever it is seems to be skilled with IT stuff. He keeps using bogus e-mail accounts, they haven't been able to track where the messages originate from because the trail keeps bouncing around and then they lose it."

That worried the hell out of him. The freaking NSA couldn't nail this sonofabitch? Not good. "This guy is careful to cover his tracks. They keep hitting dead ends everywhere they look. They're checking into the possibility it's connected to what happened in New Orleans." He prayed it didn't, but his instincts said otherwise. And his instincts were rarely wrong.

DeLuca nodded. "That's good. Anything we can do?"

"No, but thanks." Damn, he really wanted to tell them the rest of it. It would explain why he hadn't been himself the past couple days. These guys were the closest things he had to brothers.

Both men were quiet, Tuck's expression and demeanor almost identical to DeLuca's. It was kind of spooky, actually. Tuck was the logical replacement choice for DeLuca if and when their commander stepped aside, and Tuck would fit that role perfectly.

Tuck started to slide off the edge of the desk. "All right. If you decide you want to talk about anything, let me—"

"Zoe's pregnant," he blurted.

A moment of shocked silence filled the room.

Staring at him, Tuck slowly lowered himself back onto the desk, then smiled. "Wow. That's great, congratulations."

He nodded. "Thanks." Rubbing his hands up and down his thighs, he stole a glance at DeLuca. "It was a shock. We didn't plan it. I'm still trying to wrap my head around it, to be honest."

He was all mixed up inside. A little excited, a little proud, and a lot worried he didn't have what it took to be a good father. He was worried not only about screwing up his child somehow, but afraid that Zoe would leave him later on if he fucked up at fatherhood. And it felt like she didn't trust him fully, otherwise she would tell him the rest of whatever was bothering her.

"I'm happy for you guys," DeLuca murmured.

Clay looked up at him then, and caught the flash of something that seemed like pain in his commander's eyes. He mentally cursed himself. DeLuca had lost his wife, Lisa, a few years ago to a brain aneurism. She'd been pregnant with their first child—one they'd been trying a long time for.

Shit.

Clay rubbed a hand over the back of his neck. "Yeah, thanks. Sorry, man. I didn't think."

DeLuca shook his head. "Don't apologize. I really am happy for you guys. I know you're probably still in shock, but as far as surprises go, a baby is the best kind."

He was right. And Clay was a selfish asshole, looking at this like it was some kind of impending tragedy for the past two days. Becoming a parent *wasn't* an impending tragedy. DeLuca had lost the wife he loved, and even though he had Briar now, it didn't make up for the loss or take the pain away.

Clay still had Zoe and he loved her more than anything. They probably would have had kids together down the line anyway; they'd kind of talked about it once or twice in the past. This just meant their timeline was moved up. "You're right. You're totally right. Jesus, I need to get my head out of my ass."

"About freaking time. We've been saying that for how long now?" Tuck joked to DeLuca.

Clay cracked a smile. He was so freaking lucky—he already had an amazing woman, and she was going to have his baby. Hardly the end of the world, becoming a daddy.

"How's Zoe doing?" DeLuca asked.

"She's...adjusting. Big shock for her too." And he was so proud of her for how she was handling everything. His woman handled stress better than anyone, and God knew she had a lot to deal with right now. He felt guilty as shit for the way he'd reacted to the news initially, wished he could go back and redo it.

"I'll bet. Once she has time for it to sink in, I'm sure everything will go smoothly for her."

Clay thought of how DeLuca must have felt on the day he'd lost Lisa and their baby. Everything had been going fine, then boom, they were both gone. "Yeah, hope so." It made his stomach clench to think of anything happening to Zoe, or the baby. So many things could go wrong and he couldn't stop any of them.

In that moment Clay realized just how scared she must be, having this sprung on her, especially since she was the one who had to carry the baby and give birth, then bear the brunt of the responsibility for caring for it in the first few months, especially if he was called away on missions. He had to step up, make sure he *showed* her he was there for her—for her and the baby—that he was going to support her through everything.

Yeah, the timing wasn't ideal, but so what? It was time he counted his blessings instead of looking at having a baby as something to dread.

"Zo's tough, and she'll make one hell of a mom,"

Tuck said. "And you'll make one hell of a dad."

Tuck knew him better than anyone, except for Zoe. His friend's show of support meant a lot. "Thanks. Gonna do my best." And just like that it felt like a weight had been lifted from his chest. "Thanks, guys. I needed that kick in the ass." Now he was starting to become more excited than anything else.

"Happy to help," Tuck said, grinning at him. "So when's the big day?"

"May. But listen, you guys can't say anything to anyone else yet. Not until the first trimester is over. That's the way Zoe wanted it."

DeLuca nodded. "I get it. Don't worry."

Clay looked at Tuck. "Celida already knows though. Zo called her last night."

Tuck's dark blond eyebrows crashed together. "She didn't tell me a thing."

"She wasn't allowed to."

"Well, now I know, so we're even."

DeLuca leaned back in his chair. "Tell Zoe congrats from me. If you guys need anything, let me know."

Coming from a man who had lost his own wife and baby, that grabbed Clay by the throat. "Thanks. I will."

DeLuca waved a hand at him and Tuck. "Now you two get outta here and do whatever you have to do for the bachelor party so I can get some work done."

Clay rose. "You sure you don't wanna come?"

"Nah, it should be a team thing, for you guys to blow off steam without your boss there. But I'm damn sure coming to the wedding."

"You'd better," Tuck told him.

Out in the hall, Tuck closed the door and grabbed Clay's arm. "Seriously, man, congrats. This is pretty freaking awesome."

Clay inclined his head, smiled, feeling lighter inside than he had in days. "Yeah." He was going to make sure he was the kind of father his child deserved. "Just pray for me that it's a boy, okay?"

At that Tuck grinned ear-to-ear. "Sorry, brother. I think karma dictates you'll be having a little girl."

Clay's smile fell as the ramifications of that possibility hit home with the force of a sledgehammer. If he had a daughter, one day a boy would want to…do things to her. And he knew how teenage boys thought. How *guys* thought.

Fuck.

A dark scowl formed on his face. Those horny bastards weren't getting near his baby girl.

Tuck burst out laughing, his deep brown eyes twinkling. "Oh, man, it's still a fifty-fifty shot either way and you should see your face right now."

"Shut up," he muttered under his breath, and headed for the door.

If he had a little girl, he'd put the fear of God into any boy who dared to show up at their door to take her out.

****

"Have we got any more of those mozzarella bite thingies?"

Zoe glanced over at Taya as she sauntered into Celida and Tuck's gorgeous new kitchen with an empty plate. Man, these ladies could eat. Her kind of people. "I've got one more tray in the oven. Hang on."

Taya waved the offer away and grabbed for the oven mitt set on the counter, brushing her long, dark curls over one shoulder. "I'll get them."

"Thanks." Zoe moved out of her way and set about finishing the tray of finger sandwiches—the third of the afternoon—on another platter.

Celida and Tuck's newly remodeled house was the

perfect place for this impromptu ladies' get together. Plenty of room for everyone to hang out, and the bright white country kitchen was a cook's dream, complete with new stainless steel appliances and black granite countertops. It opened up into the rest of the great room, giving the entire space a bright, airy feel. The view out the French doors that led out to the patio showed off the gorgeous wood deck and manicured backyard. Clay and Tuck had worked on it together.

Zoe smiled as she remembered catching sight of him once out there this past summer, wearing nothing but jeans, boots and a leather tool belt, all those gorgeous muscles in his upper body on display for her.

She'd wanted to ravage him on the spot, but had been forced to wait until they got into the truck later. Clay had laughed when she'd jumped him in the front seat…until she'd jerked his fly down and freed him from his boxer briefs. Then he'd been too busy getting his world rocked to do anything but grip her hips and growl in pleasure.

Tendrils of heat licked deep in her belly at the memory. She cleared her throat. Things were way better now that she'd mostly come clean to him the other night. She might even bring up the marriage thing soon, see how it went. Maybe after Tuck and Celida's wedding. Once he saw his best friend get married, maybe the idea wouldn't scare him so much anymore. "How we doing for wine out there, do you know?"

"Just opened a fifth bottle of white and we're still on our second red, I think." Taya eyed her. "You haven't touched yours and it's gotta be warm by now. You want something else instead?"

Zoe glanced at her still full wine glass she'd set by the sink, which she had no intention of drinking. She'd only taken it to avoid curious looks and questions about why she wasn't drinking. "Yeah, actually. Maybe some herbal tea or something. Celida should have some peppermint up in the cupboard, if you don't mind."

"Not at all." Taya reached up on tiptoe to look for the tea in the cupboard Zoe indicated, grabbed a box and looked back at her. "You feeling okay? You've barely eaten anything."

It was really hard to lie right to this woman's face. Taya was sweet and caring beyond belief and Zoe had fallen in love with her exactly three seconds after meeting Schroder's incredibly strong and loving lady. Still, she wasn't going to say anything about the baby.

"Yeah, just been busy in here and my stomach's a little off, that's all."

Taya filled the electric kettle and turned it on, frowning. "You worried about the messages you've been getting?"

Zoe nodded, appreciating Taya's insight and concern. "Yeah. I know the FBI and NSA have people looking into it, so that makes me feel better." Although they still had yet to come up with an actual list of suspects. "And I'm being careful. I don't leave my place alone, Clay made me promise. He dropped me off here before he left to get the stuff for their party tonight. Plus I'm armed with pepper spray and a taser."

Between the news about the baby and wondering how things would go with Clay when the marriage thing came up, the pregnancy hormones, her stupid stalker and her looming deadline that was coming up way too fast, it was no wonder her stomach was upset.

"That's good." Taya put a teabag into a mug she'd found.

Zoe paused in filling the platter and aimed a smile at her new friend. She refused to dwell on her stresses right now. Today was about celebrating love and friendship, forging a stronger bond with her new friends. And she felt a kind of inner glow, knowing a baby was snuggled safely inside her body. "I'm really glad you and Schroder found each other again."

Taya smiled back. "Me too. It's funny how life works, isn't it?"

"No kidding." Taking two steps toward her, Zoe wrapped her arms around Taya and hugged her. The gang was getting used to her displays of affection, with the exception of maybe Briar, DeLuca's lady, who was still a little standoffish and didn't seem to know what to make of her.

Zoe didn't take it personally though. Briar hadn't had an easy life and it took a while for her to trust people. Zoe was getting there though, slowly but surely. Briar hadn't stiffened up like a poker this time when Zoe had hugged her on the doorstep earlier. Major progress.

"I'm so lucky to have you ladies in my life. Who else would understand how crazy our men are?" Zoe didn't know Marisol and Carmela that well yet either, but they were both friendly so she knew it wouldn't be long before they were all friends. That support network was vital when their men had such dangerous jobs.

Taya squeezed her in return, her calm energy like a balm to Zoe's anxious mind. "For real." The kettle popped. Taya released her and poured the boiling water over the teabag. "Want honey in it or anything?"

"No thanks. Straight up is good."

Taya handed her the mug with a grin, the bright overhead light catching the fine scars on the left side of her face and throat. "So hardcore, drinking peppermint tea straight up."

"I know, right?" She grabbed the full platter. "Better take this out to the starving masses before they start gnawing on the furniture."

Out in the living room, all the girls were sitting on the couches or on cushions on the floor. Zoe considered it a minor miracle that she'd been able to wrangle everyone here at the same time—during the middle of a weekday, no less—but the sight filled her with happiness.

Since moving from New Orleans she'd missed her friends, but these women were becoming more than that. They were becoming her sisters. And every single one of them knew they could reach out to any of them for help, an understanding ear or someone to vent to. Living with a stubborn alpha male resulted in some occasional…frustrations that only another woman in the same situation could ever understand.

The only notable exception was Summer, Blackwell's wife. Zoe had yet to meet her, and she wondered why Summer never seemed to show up for team functions. Clay had told her their marriage seemed to be on the rocks, but Zoe was more than a little curious about the Defense Intelligence Agency agent.

"More dainty, crustless tea sandwiches for y'all," she announced, sauntering over to place the platter in the middle of the already cluttered coffee table. They'd devoured everything else so far, leaving nothing but crumbs and messy finger napkins.

"Oh, you got the cucumber ones!" Celida exclaimed, reaching out from her perch in the center of the largest sofa to snatch three of them.

Zoe laughed at her. "I wanted to get whole wheat bread at least, but the caterer seemed totally offended by the request. Thus, you got your unhealthy white bread."

Celida made a humming noise as she chewed the little dainty, her eyes sparkling. "Delish."

Taya came up behind her and added the platter of mozzarella bites to the table, a chilled bottle of white in her other hand. "Who needs more wine?"

A chorus of requests sounded and five wine glasses appeared before her.

Zoe snickered and looked at Taya. "I'll go open another couple of bottles."

Two hours and another few bottles of wine later, Zoe

leaned back into the sofa cushions and glanced around the room with a smile. This was exactly what she'd needed. Good food, camaraderie and friendship.

Rachel, Evers's other half, reached out and plucked Celida's mostly empty glass from her fingers, pushing her long brown hair over one shoulder. "That won't do. Somebody give the bride-to-be a refill, quick."

"I'm on it." Carmela, Vance's woman who they'd all just met, jumped up and grabbed the only remaining bottle of wine, filled Celida's glass nearly to the top. Zoe liked her already.

Celida grimaced. "I really shouldn't, but...okay."

"Don't forget you've still got to be able to stand upright on your own for the dress fitting in an hour," Zoe reminded her in a dry voice.

Celida scoffed. "I'm a former Marine, don't forget. Couple glasses of wine got nothing on me. And you can drive us there."

"Aww, you guys are leaving?" Marisol—Cruzie's better half—asked, popping another bite-sized appetizer into her mouth. She was a doll, and freaking smart. A fellow lawyer, like Zoe had been until she'd taken up writing full time.

"Just for a little while. Y'all are staying until we get back, right? Because I've got a small mountain of desserts waiting in the fridge," Zoe said, pointing a thumb toward the kitchen. She slid a glance toward Briar. "Including a tray of freshly baked baklava." Zoe knew they were her favorite, because a certain HRT commander had told her so. She was determined to win Briar over, no matter what it took, and she wasn't above bribing her with sweets to make it happen.

Briar gave her a mock scowl, narrowed her black eyes. "Damn you. My one weakness."

"Oh, I don't know about that. I hear your only real weakness is a five-eleven stud with a pair of dreamy green eyes. And I also hear he's pretty good with a sniper rifle, too, as luck would have it. *Hot*."

A blush crept into Briar's bronze-toned cheeks. "Yeah, he's not bad." Then she grinned, and it was pure sass. "Almost as good as me."

Everyone snickered and hooted at that, and Zoe smiled as the conversation swirled around the room once again. The woman fascinated her. She absolutely planned to base a future character on her, wanted to ask her a million questions but knew Briar would be way too uncomfortable with that.

Zoe didn't have security clearance so she wasn't sure of the exact details, but from what she'd managed to pry out of Clay about Briar, he'd made her sound like some sort of a badass female assassin. Whatever Briar had done in the past—or maybe was still doing—Clay clearly thought she was amazeballs.

Zoe eyed her now, sitting there on the couch, contained and almost removed from what was going on around her. She looked younger than she actually was, and despite whatever lethal skillset she had there was an almost innocent air about her. A real mystery.

Just the kind that Zoe loved to write about. And now that most of her personal stress with Clay had been resolved, she was feeling eager to hit the keyboard again, finish up this latest book. She even had an idea of how it ended, with the heroine demonstrating her absolute trust in the hero. Trust was the most critical part of any relationship's foundation, and she regretted ever questioning Clay's character.

A while later she glanced at her watch. "Okay, woman, you're done." She plucked Celida's wine glass from her hand. "Time to get our inner divas on and squeeze into our fabulous dresses."

The shop owner was staying after hours as a favor to Celida. Zoe hoped the bust of her gown would still fit her.

They'd go to the dress place first for the fitting, then to the hairdresser for a consultation.

Celida was one of the most low-maintenance women Zoe had ever met, but she refused to let her bestie show up to her own wedding without looking like she'd stepped off the pages of a bridal magazine.

Celida pushed to her feet and pointed at the group, turning in a half circle to aim a warning finger at each of them in turn. "You guys better still be here when we get back."

"We might be persuaded to stay." Taya flopped back against the couch she sat on and draped a friendly arm around Carmela's shoulders, her message clear. The ladies were enjoying themselves and weren't going anywhere for the next couple hours. "Hurry back though, or we can't promise there'll be any dessert left."

"Don't you dare eat up all the dark chocolate stuff then," Celida warned with a mock scowl. "Because I will take you bitches *down*."

Zoe smothered a laugh. "And with that you are officially cut off," she said, turning her friend by the shoulders and steering her toward the doorway off the kitchen that led to the garage.

Chapter Seven

S he'd done it. She'd found her.

Amanda's heart raced as she sped toward the freeway entrance. She'd gotten lucky ten minutes ago when one of her contacts got a hit on the government license plate from the car SA Celida Morales had been driving yesterday. After identifying it on CCTV footage he'd called immediately—because that bitch Zoe was with her.

She gripped the phone tight as she drove. They had to get to the dress shop before the women left. "Are you on your way?" she asked Dominic.

"Yeah." She could hear traffic sounds in the background and knew he was on the road. "I'll probably beat you there by a couple minutes. I'm bringing our diversion."

If he meant what she thought he did, then it was freaking awesome. She didn't want to say too much over the phone though, just in case someone had managed to figure out her identity and was trying to track her.

"Good. I'll meet you at the rendezvous point."

Elation zinged through her. So close now. Everything was finally coming together—if they could just get to the dress shop in time. Dominic would be bringing the heavy weaponry but she had two pistols with her, just in case.

Even if everything went sideways before and after the diversion, she should still be able to get Zoe in the confusion that would follow. She and Dominic had planned this out carefully, had gone over several backup plans.

Amanda had purposely made it look like a man had been stalking Zoe this whole time. Dominic would flush Zoe into the trap Amanda would spring. Then Zoe's lover would come for her.

Then, together, she and Dom would carry out the hit that would earn them their huge payday.

She and Dominic had to act fast. There was a chance someone had put the pieces together and figured out that Zoe was being targeted. And if Clay Bauer wasn't already coming for her, he would be soon enough.

Her pulse skipped. There'd be no reward money without killing one of the HRT members, so this plan had to work. Amanda would take Zoe to a secluded place so Bauer could watch her die when he showed up. Zoe was both a means to an end, and a personal score to settle.

She wanted to watch that bitch suffer first, for meddling in other people's business and getting Carlos killed. When Bauer showed up for her—and he would show up—Amanda wanted see the agony on his face before Dominic ended him too. The diversion and disguises would allow them the perfect opportunity to make it all happen.

Amanda smiled to herself and drove as fast as she dared to the exit she needed. After the deed was done it would take the authorities a while to follow the threads of the investigation and figure out she had planned this op.

By then she'd be safely ensconced in the non-extradition country she'd chosen, awaiting her wire transfer payment from Fuentes's people to an offshore account she'd set up. She would get her house on the beach, spend her days basking in her slice of tropical paradise. Fuentes had a reputation for paying what he promised. As soon as his people confirmed she was responsible for the hit, she'd be set up for the rest of her life.

She stole a quick glance at herself in the rearview mirror, satisfied with what she saw. No one would bat an eyelash if they saw her walking down the sidewalk toward the dress shop, especially not in her stolen cop uniform. No one would question her carrying a weapon in the holster on her hip.

And no one would question her helping a frightened citizen in the aftermath of the terrifying incident that was about to take place, she thought with a smug grin.

****

It was quiet over in enemy territory, but Clay knew they were out there, hiding less than a hundred yards away in the dried-up rows of cornstalks. "You ladies too scared to come out, or what?" he taunted. "Is there a maze in there you got lost in? Or maybe you found a baseball diamond?"

"If you build it, they will come," Evers mocked, hunkered down beside him.

"Says the leader of the pussies hiding behind a barricade!" Cruz yelled back.

"Whatever, Cruzie. We took you out, like, ten minutes ago, so you're supposed to be dead anyhow," Clay called out from behind the cover of the barricade he'd constructed of old tires earlier.

"Fuck you, they're just flesh wounds," Cruzie shot back from somewhere across the empty cornfield. "I'm still in the fight. Man up and come out from behind your little hiding place over there, and I'll show you. Got a round waiting here with your name on it."

With an evil chuckle Clay nudged Evers. "He's so easy to rile."

Evers snickered in delight. "I know. All that passionate, Puerto Rican blood, I guess." He added his voice to the trash talk. "Come on, you chicken shits, get out here and meet your paintball makers like men."

"Brave talk, coming from a bunch of pussies cowering behind the only real cover out here," Tuck fired back.

"*Smart* pussies," Clay countered, immensely pleased with himself.

"Whatever man, you were the one who put that thing there in the first place last night, so you knew exactly where it was all along. Totally unfair tactical advantage," Blackwell accused.

Clay grinned, loving everything about this. He hadn't had this much fun in a long time. Well, he definitely had fun with Zoe, but it was a different, private and extremely fucking hot kind of fun. He shifted his grip on his weapon, itching to attack. "Come out and tell me that to my face, Blackwell."

"You show me yours, I'll show you mine," his teammate answered.

He turned to Evers. "Whaddya think? Should we go for it?"

Evers shrugged. "Why not? I'm starving. Let's get this over with so we can eat."

He looked past Evers to Vance, who was at a distinct disadvantage with his right arm strapped across his chest. "What about you, man?"

"I could eat a whole freaking cow by myself right now man, and those steaks are smelling pretty damn good to me."

"Yeah. Okay then. On three." He faced the edge of the pile of tires again and called out to the enemy team. "All right, you pansy-asses. Let's do this. *Molòn labé*." A classic expression of defiance that loosely translated to *come get some, motherfuckers*. That King Leonidas must have had titanium balls when he'd said that to the Persians at Thermopylae.

"Bring it, assholes! We're ready," Tuck answered.

"Wait, so we're going Rambo mode?" Evers asked.

"Rambo on steroids," Clay responded. "Three," he called out to the others. "Two. Go!"

Roaring their battle cries, Clay and his two teammates rushed out from behind cover just as Tuck and his team emerged from the dried cornstalks.

Immediately they opened up on each other, firing everything they had. Whoops and war cries filled the night, along with the rapid *thunk-thunk-thunk* of hundreds of paintballs finding their targets.

Rounds hit Clay in the torso, the arms. One smashed into his right cheekbone, and then someone played dirty and began firing straight at his groin.

Since he'd been smart enough to wear a cup the impacts didn't put him into the fetal position like they would have without protection, but he still roared and turned to face his attacker. In the light of the fire behind him in the fire pit he saw Schroder running straight for him, cackling like a maniac as he fired round after round right between Clay's legs.

Clay lowered himself to Schroder's level and returned the favor, firing until his weapon was empty. Schroder hit the ground and cupped his balls, groaning as the rest of Clay's shots slapped into his prostrate body.

"Bet you wish you had a cup on right now, huh, Doc?" he yelled over the noise.

Schroder groaned and tried to sit up, something that sounded a lot like "freaking asshole" coming from the team medic. Clay laughed, unrepentant.

Everyone emptied their magazines on their enemies. Seconds later the volume of fire died down, then stopped altogether, the entire team grinning like idiots and covered in paint.

With all the ammo fired, the game came to an abrupt end. Everyone lowered their paintball guns and raised their goggles. In the light of the campfire the extent of the carnage was visible.

All seven of them were covered from head to toe in bright yellow or blue splotches. The spot over Clay's right cheekbone was swelling where Schroder's round had hit. Would make Tuck and Celida's wedding photos memorable.

"Man, that was *fun*," Tuck exclaimed. "Best bachelor party ever, Bauer."

He shrugged. "I try." It was pretty tame compared to what his fellow SEALs had done to guys once the team found out one of them was getting married or had eloped. Clay had helped kidnap one teammate the day after the guy eloped—he'd done it without telling anyone in an effort to spare himself the physical punishment he knew he would have suffered once the team found out.

They'd tied him up anyway, shaved off his eyebrows and pubic hair, thrown him into the back of a van, then driven out into the middle of the California desert and dumped him there. All in good fun, of course.

So really, Tuck was getting off easy.

"And hey, team with least number of hits on them wins," Clay announced, quickly turning to count the marks on each of his teammates. "Evers, turn around for a minute."

"Whatever," Schroder scoffed, immediately swiping his gloved hands over the front of himself, smearing the paint everywhere. "Now try and count how many times I was hit, frogman."

"About twenty times in the nuts alone, I'm pretty sure," he answered.

Schroder's lips quirked and he held up a middle finger. "Sit on it and rotate, man."

"You're not my type, sorry. And you're also a total loss," Clay remarked, ignoring him to keep counting how many hits Evers had on him. "And as there's not enough left of you to identify, guess we'll have to use DNA to confirm before we can inform Taya what happened to you."

The guys laughed, and even though this was just a game, Clay was too competitive to stop counting and moved on to Vance. "Ha! Sixty-two," he declared when he was finished, looking at Tuck in triumph. "What about your guys?"

In answer, Tuck stared right back and smeared the paint on the front of his body too.

Clay pumped his fist in the air. "We win!"

Schroder rolled his eyes. "Yeah, Bauer, your team wins. And your dicks are much bigger than ours too."

"Damn right," he said with a cocky smile. *And it turns out my boys are expert swimmers too, just like me*, he thought with a smug grin. Yeah, he was starting to feel pretty damn proud about becoming a daddy now. He was looking forward to telling the rest of the guys when it was time.

Everyone dumped their gear into a pile and gathered around the fire pit, setting up the folding lawn chairs in a circle. When everyone had a cold beer in hand from one of the coolers, Clay set about checking on the steaks. Schroder ambled over, beer can in hand, face covered in paint. "Need some help?"

"There's no bacon, if that's what you were hoping for," Clay told him.

Schroder laughed softly. "Well maybe I was hoping a little." He eyed the steaks on the grill. "Those'll do though. Smells awesome."

"Glad to hear it. They're almost done. Tuck likes his medium rare, so give him this, will you?" He scooped the steak up off the grill with his tongs and added a baked potato. He wasn't much of a cook, but every guy could figure out how to grill meat. "Evers put the butter and everything else on the table over there." He nodded to the table he'd set next to the coolers earlier.

"I like mine medium-well, in case you were wondering," Schroder answered over his shoulder as he went to serve the groom-to-be.

Clay and Vance manned the grill to finish everything up, and when everyone had a plate and were seated around the fire, Clay stood and held up his beer. "A toast, to the groom-to-be."

He paused, searched for something appropriate to say. He wasn't nearly as cynical about marriage as he'd been before meeting Zoe, but that didn't mean he couldn't still tease the hell out of Tuck. "Good luck."

Everyone started laughing, then a chorus of "good lucks" rang out around the fire. Tuck took it good-naturedly, grinning as he saluted him with his own beer. "Thanks, boys. But I don't need luck because I know she's the only woman who could ever handle me."

A chorus of whistles and catcalls broke out. Smiling, Clay took a seat and dug into his steak and baked potato. Three bites in, his phone rang.

Pulling it from his back pocket, he stilled when he saw Alex Rycroft's number. Had to be about Zoe's stalker.

He put his plate aside and stood, quickly walking away from the group while he answered. "Bauer."

"Hey. I just got some new intel on the stalker situation."

Clay kept his back to the group, plugged his free ear to hear better. "Okay, shoot."

"My people have been looking into this and a few of the possible suspects they've come up with are flagged in our system."

Clay's hand tightened around the phone. "Okay."

"Based on what they've compiled thus far, I'd say this is definitely connected to what happened in NOLA."

Clay set his jaw. *Fuck.* He'd been afraid of this. It tore him up that he wasn't with her now, that he couldn't get to her immediately. "How so?"

"We're following up leads right now, but it looks like there's a possible connection here to a Fuentes enforcer."

At that the blood drained out of Clay's face. He spun around and rushed back toward the others. He needed to get to Zoe. "Who?" he grated out.

"We're not sure on that either. But there's enough evidence to suggest that Fuentes has offered a reward for a hit on one of you guys. And we think someone's targeting Zoe to get to you."

He grabbed his keys with his free hand, fisted them so tight his knuckles ached. The idea that some asshole was targeting Zoe to get to him or one of the other guys clawed at him like razor wire. She'd been through hell once already and now she was carrying his baby...

He couldn't imagine losing them, the way DeLuca had lost his wife and child. Clay would do anything to protect her.

"How much is the reward?"

"One million."

Jesus. He didn't even care how Fuentes was managing to pull those kinds of strings from behind maximum-security bars. "So someone knew about what happened in NOLA and they've been tracking her through her pen name to get to me or one of the other guys."

"Looks like." Rycroft's voice was grim. "I've got a new inside source helping us out, so all this intel is credible. But what about Zoe, does she have security on her?"

Clay's steps faltered. Ah, shit, the bridal shower. He stopped. "She's with Celida, and I know Celida will be armed. But all the guys' women are together at Tuck's place right now." That was one big fucking target for a narco-terrorist looking to make him and the guys come running.

Nausea swirled in his belly, his muscles bunching tight.

"Get them out, or at least hide them until we can safely evacuate them."

"I'm on it. Thanks, man, but I gotta go."

"Okay. Let me know if you need anything."

"Yeah." Clay hung up and immediately dialed Zoe, his heart beating a staccato rhythm against his chest wall as he looked back to the others. The guys were all sitting around eating and bullshitting, totally unaware of the threat hovering over the girls.

He held the phone to his ear, marched toward his teammates. Zoe should be at the shower right now, but she had mentioned running more wedding-related errands with Celida after. God dammit...

Answer, Zo. Pick up the damn phone.

Her phone went to voicemail.

He swore, left her a text and rushed back to the fire pit. When they saw him everyone stopped talking, six pairs of eyes locked on him in utter silence.

He focused on Tuck. "I need you to call Celida. Find out if she's with Zoe."

Tuck stood, frowning at Clay's urgent tone and reached for his phone. "Everything okay?"

"No." He wanted the others to hear this too. They needed to know about the threat. "Rycroft called to say he's pretty sure a former Fuentes enforcer is the one who's been stalking Zoe."

Tuck's face tightened. "He's sure?"

"Yes." Clay looked at the others. "Somehow Fuentes has put a hit out on us. Whoever's been stalking Zoe is after the reward money offered. If this asshole knows where she is, he'll go after her."

"Holy shit," Cruzie muttered. "What if he knows they're all together at Tuck's right now?" All the others tensed, watching Clay.

Yeah, it was a fucking nightmare.

The others began fishing out their phones, the urgency palpable.

Tuck was waiting for Celida to pick up, but a moment later shook his head. "Voicemail." A second later he began snapping out a series of commands to Celida, warning her about the situation.

Clay's gaze snapped to the others. "Everybody, alert your girl and find out where Zoe is."

Everyone was already on their phones, but Vance was the first one to get the intel they needed. "Carm says Celida and Zoe left forty minutes ago to go get their dresses fitted."

Shit. Clay looked at Tuck. "Know which one?"

"Hang on." Tuck was scrolling through something on his phone.

He looked at the others, who were all watching him, phones to their ears. "Tell the girls to stay at Tuck's place and get down to the basement."

Since this fucker had been specifically targeting Zoe so far the other women might not be at risk, but she'd been with them earlier and Clay's guys wouldn't take chances with their safety. The basement would hopefully provide enough cover if someone had been able to track them there.

"Hell," Vance muttered, and began rattling out instructions to Carmela.

Clay dialed Zoe again, the murmur of voices floated around him as he watched Tuck, urging him to hurry.

No answer from Zoe.

Cursing, he lowered the phone. "Tuck. Where?" In his peripheral he could already see Vance and Schroder dousing the fire with the ice and water from the coolers.

"It's…Debutante Dresses," Tuck said, and quickly read out the address. "I'm calling there now."

"Let's go." To the others, Clay added, "Go to Tuck's place and get the girls home safely. Everyone report back to me or Tuck when you get home. And watch your sixes. This asshole is gunning for us."

Without waiting for a response he turned and ran for his truck. Dread coiled inside him, the seconds ticking past way too fast. He and Tuck had to get to Zoe and Celida before whoever was hunting them got there first.

Chapter Eight

A manda tugged the brim of her police hat down farther over her forehead and exited the car she'd rented with a fake ID and matching credit card. After driving past the dress shop a minute ago and seeing Agent Morales's car parked at the curb out front, she knew Celida and Zoe were both still in there.

Hurry, her instinct urged her.

Her pulse picked up, her hands growing clammy inside her pockets as she moved closer to her unsuspecting targets. The sidewalks here were fairly quiet, most of the businesses having shut down a few hours earlier. On this block only the dress shop and a combination bookstore-coffee shop were still open.

She walked the half block north to the rendezvous point. Dominic was nowhere in sight. She was just reaching for her cell phone when it dinged with an incoming text. Dominic.

Ahead of you. Twenty yards.

Glancing up, she saw some vehicles parked down the street along the curb, behind an ambulance. A split second later the ambulance driver's door popped open and Dominic stepped out wearing a paramedic's uniform.

Amanda stopped in her tracks, a wide smile spreading across her face. *Perfect.* "Hey."

He shut the ambulance door and walked over to her. When he got close enough he signaled for her to follow with a nod of his head. Out of the light cast by the streetlamps lining the sidewalk, he bent his head and murmured, "This is a CCTV black spot. Here." He passed her an earpiece.

She pretended to tuck a lock of hair behind her ear, tucked the earpiece in place and tested it. "Did you find your site yet?" she whispered back, keeping an eye on the sidewalk. It wasn't unusual to see a cop talking to a paramedic, so she didn't think they'd drawn any notice from passersby yet.

"Check," he said with a nod to indicate his earpiece was working. "And wouldn't you know it, there's a handicap parking spot right out front of the shop." His voice was clear in her earpiece as well.

"I saw that. All the blinds at the front of the shop are open, too."

"Makes my job so much easier," he said with a sly smile that sent a rush of arousal through her.

She looked up and down the street once. No one was even walking in the area. "So you'll go park out front and then get set up?"

They'd decided a sniper shot from another location would give them the most leeway in terms of escape options. If they went into the shop to attack, security cameras there and along the street would capture their every move and the NSA's state-of-the-art facial recognition software would ID them in a matter of minutes. They'd be caught the instant they showed up for their flights.

The sniper plan was best. Once word got out that

there was an active shooter in the area, everything would go on lockdown.

"I've already stashed my gear. I'll park out front then double back and get in position."

They'd gone over a few options but she'd left it up to him to choose his hide site. "Where?" she asked, watching his eyes. Deep, dark brown. Nearly black. Like Carlos's had been.

She shook the thought away. Her recent online activity increased the pressure on them. There was a chance someone was onto them already. And after this the FBI would issue a city-wide manhunt, making their getaway window tight.

She'd have to be smart, keep a low profile when she fled. This was risky, but taking the lion's share of a million bucks was too much temptation.

"Bakery across the street. I already disabled the security system."

Oh yeah, skilled *and* deadly, like Carlos had been. A pang of grief hit her. God, she missed him so much. Probably always would. Zoe would suffer for taking him from her.

"How long do you need to set up?" In the meantime she'd have to make sure Zoe and Celida didn't leave the shop before Dom was ready. If they started to leave Dom would alert her. Having Celida there complicated matters. Amanda couldn't simply go in and take Zoe herself with a trained agent there. She'd have to wait for Dom to flush them out the back.

"Five minutes."

Excited butterflies fluttered in her stomach. *So close.* "Works for me. You'll let me know if you need help lining it up?"

"Yes."

She gave him a cocky smile. "I'll be waiting. See you later."

As soon as it was done she'd pick him up at the prearranged meeting spot and wait for Bauer. After that, she'd get the hell out of town. They had other disguises, fake passports and other ID to help them slip out of the country. She knew how to do it. People within Alvarez's circle had taught her. She'd already booked a last-minute flight out of the country using one of her aliases before arriving here.

Turning on her heel, she crossed the street and headed up the sidewalk back toward the dress shop, the weight of her pistols reassuring her, helping her believe that everything was going to work out. One rested in its holster on her hip, her backup weapon strapped to her calf beneath the pant leg of her uniform. When she glanced over her shoulder, Dominic was already gone, having vanished into the shadows like the ghost he was.

Nerves and adrenaline mixed with excitement, sending a rush of endorphins through her veins.

A buzz of anticipation tingled in her stomach, her rubber-soled boots quiet on the pavement. They were as prepared as they were going to get. All that was left to do was execute the plan. A few more minutes and she'd finally secure what she needed to start the life she deserved.

****

"Still no answer from Celida or the shop." Tuck's voice was rife with frustration as he lowered his phone.

Zoe either. Worry was eating a hole in his gut. "We're still ten minutes out," Clay said. Dammit, of all the freaking times for Zoe and Celida not to be monitoring their phones. "That's too long. Find out if any of our people are in the area. Maybe they can get the girls out. The cops are gonna beat us there, so make sure they know to search the area for a shooter." They'd called for police backup immediately after figuring out where Zoe and Celida were.

Tuck grunted by way of answer, already on the phone to someone else. Clay knew his buddy didn't need instructions on how to handle this, but he wanted to be sure they were on the same page. He pressed down harder on the accelerator while Tuck spoke to someone else. Sounded like it might be Travers, Celida's partner.

Clay swerved around another pickup, tailgated another car and laid on his horn until the driver pulled into the slow lane, ignoring the driver's flung up middle finger. He had a bad feeling about this, real bad. The enforcer was out there right now, hunting Zoe, and trying to lure Clay into the trap he'd created.

A trap he had no choice but to walk into, no matter the risk to himself. And unfortunately Tuck and Celida were caught up in it now too.

Up ahead the traffic snarled around what appeared to be some kind of road construction. Cursing under his breath, Clay jerked the wheel and headed down a side alley. A garbage truck blocked the way halfway down.

Fuck.

He threw it into reverse, gunned it back the way he'd come, the muscles in his arms so tight it felt like the tendons might snap. Reaching the street, he did a J-turn, cranking the wheel hard to the right to spin the front of the truck around to the left, then shifted to drive as it spun and shot forward back into traffic.

"Up there," Tuck urged, pointing up and to the left.

Clay saw the opening he indicated and gunned it. He swerved around oncoming traffic, turned hard to the left and careened around another vehicle coming the other way. Just as quickly, another blocked their way.

An old man, squinting in the glare of Clay's headlights. He raised one hand to shade his eyes.

Clay snarled and laid on the horn. "Get the fuck outta

the way," he yelled at the other driver, uncaring that he wouldn't hear him.

The old man jumped, waved his hands in either apology or surrender and gingerly began backing his car down the narrow side street.

"Come on, come *on*," Clay growled, knuckles white as he gripped the wheel.

The instant the old man moved his car enough, Clay hit the gas, streaking past the other vehicle with a squeal of tires. This congestion was killing him, might cost Zoe her life. He had to get to the freeway, had to make up for lost time.

Neither he nor Tuck spoke as he fought his way to the nearest onramp, only the sounds of the engine racing and the occasional blare of a horn as they sped past someone. Gripping the wheel tight Clay kept his focus pinned on the road in front of him, desperate to get to Zoe. Finally he reached the road to the onramp.

The engine's pitch grew higher as he pressed harder on the accelerator. The speedometer's needle read fifty miles per hour. Sixty. Seventy. He took the onramp at seventy-five, increased it to eight-five, then ninety.

It still wasn't fast enough. His heart thudded against his ribcage, a frantic rhythm borne of fear.

Zoe. Please be safe, baby.

Tuck remained silent in the passenger seat, no doubt lost in his own worry for both his cousin and Celida. The tension in the truck was palpable. Clay clenched his jaw and raced down the darkened freeway, zipping in and out to dodge slower moving traffic, feeling the seconds slip past with agonizing speed.

Zoe had to be okay, he told himself. The enforcer planned to use her to lure him to the pickup point, and he was going there no matter what. He'd vowed to her that he'd never let her down, that he wouldn't let anything happen to her.

He'd do anything to save Zoe. Even die for her.

****

Zoe winced and tugged futilely at the bodice of the gown to try and squeeze her boobs into the cups for the second attempt. It was no good; her girls were spilling out everywhere. And they freaking *hurt*.

"Well?" Celida called from outside the change room. "What's the verdict?"

"Clay's definitely going to be happy about this latest development," she answered. A whole cup size up already, at least. She'd noticed some of her bras getting tight but until the pregnancy bombshell she hadn't thought anything of it.

Celida laughed. "All right, well get out here and let's see if Sophie can figure out some kind of magical solution."

The shop phone rang again in the background but the owner ignored it. Maybe because it was after hours and she'd only kept the shop open for Zoe and Celida.

Holding the chiffon-covered bodice with the built-in bra over her chest, Zoe opened the door and stepped out. Celida's and Sophie's gazes both zeroed in on the problem area.

"Oh, my, that's…my," Sophie murmured, putting a hand to her chest.

Yeah. Her girls were looking pretty impressive at the moment.

"She got knocked up a few weeks ago," Celida joked.

"Oh, well. Congratulations?" Sophie definitely posed that more as a question than a compliment.

"Thanks," Zoe said, unfazed by Celida's teasing. "So, do you think you can do anything about this?" She glanced down at her swollen boobs. They looked pretty awesome, if she did say so herself. Sucked that they were too damn sore for her and Clay to enjoy them to the fullest.

Sophie pursed her lips as she pondered that for a moment. "I could try and add a panel or some lacing to the back, maybe…" She stepped forward and turned Zoe by the shoulders, gripped the two halves at the back of the gown. "Yes, I think just adding an extra piece of material on either side of the zipper would do it."

"What about the built-in bra cups?" Zoe asked. "I'm coming out of them all over the place."

Celida snickered. "Bauer must be in heaven."

Zoe shot her a grin. "Side perk." She looked back at Sophie. "Well?"

"I think I'll take out the bra entirely. If we pull it in enough here," she said, tugging the material snug across Zoe's ribcage, "it'll give you more room up top and you won't feel so squashed."

"Okay, but make sure it's snug enough to hold me in tight. I'm so sore right now there's no way I could handle them flopping around all day in this thing."

Celida burst out laughing at the description. "Gotta love you, Zo. You are one of a kind."

"That's right, and don't you forget it."

"As if I ever could." She shot Zoe a fond grin. "Okay, so no worries then. My dress is still good to go, so only this one alteration needed." To Sophie she added, "You can have this done by Saturday afternoon, right?"

The woman's eyes widened slightly at the two-day deadline, but her expression smoothed out and she nodded. "Sure. There will be an extra charge for that, of course."

"That's fine."

Sophie smiled. "I'll take care of it right away."

"Great."

After standing there for a few minutes more while

Sophie marked the material and put pins in place, Zoe wandered back into the change room to put her own clothes on. She checked her phone on the way out to meet Celida at the front counter, frowned. Clay had left three texts and called her multiple times since she'd been here.

Call me back ASAP, the last one read.

"Something's up with Clay," she said to her friend, coming to stand at the cash register. Outside the large front window to her right it was already dark.

"Lord, if one of them got injured during the freaking paintball game, DeLuca will not be happy."

"No doubt."

"Could you fill this in please?" Sophie asked her, sliding a piece of paper across the desk toward her. "I need your contact info on file, just in case."

"Sure." Only half paying attention to Sophie as she slid a pen to her, Zoe cleared the screen and started to dial Clay's number. The pen fell off the edge of the counter. Zoe bent to pick it up.

Glass cracked behind her and something thunked into the wall behind the desk.

"Down!" Celida yelled before Zoe could react and grabbed her, tackled her to the floor.

Zoe hit hard on her stomach, heart hammering. What the hell? Had someone just *shot* at them?

"*Move*, Zo." Celida shoved her hip, pushing her toward the only cover close by, a concrete pillar.

Adrenaline shot through her. Zoe scrambled to her hands and knees and scurried around the edge of the pillar. She gasped when another round slammed into the back of it, spraying bits of concrete around her. It was too thin. It wasn't enough.

"Shit," Celida muttered, service pistol in one hand, the other fumbling for her phone as she crouched in front of Zoe. "Sophie's down."

With her back to the pillar and too afraid to move,

Zoe risked a peek over her shoulder. She just barely caught sight of Sophie, slumped against the wall with a hand to the center of her chest, blood spilling into a puddle around her. Her wide blue eyes were locked on Zoe, full of terror, her mouth open as she gasped, blood dribbling down her chin.

Hit in the lung.

"Sophie, don't move," Zoe ordered, her breathing erratic.

"Asshole has to be shooting at us from across the street," Celida muttered, "and with the lights on that window gives him a clear view of every move we make."

The back of Zoe's neck prickled. She could feel the crosshairs lining up on the pillar again. If she moved, she'd be dead.

Celida began rattling off information to whom Zoe assumed was a 911 operator.

"B-blinds…"

Squeezed into as small a target as possible, Zoe snapped her head around to stare at Sophie. "What?"

The woman tried to lift her free hand, weakly pointed it toward something hidden under the desk she was hidden behind. "B-button."

Zoe's gaze shot to the blinds pulled to either side of the front window, then back to Sophie. Celida was right. They were fish in a barrel right now. "There's a button to activate the blinds?"

Sophie managed a nod, her hand falling to her side. More blood spilled from the wound in her chest, dripped from her mouth. She began to wheeze.

The sound made her skin crawl. "I'm going to shut the blinds," Zoe said to Celida, who was still on the phone trying to get them backup.

She shook her head. "No, don't move."

"You keep reporting. I gotta help Sophie and get us some real cover," Zoe snapped, gingerly getting to her knees while staying with her back to the pillar. Sophie was dying right in front of them. Closing those blinds was their only chance.

"Zoe, *no*."

Her mind was already made up. Zoe got into a crouch and gauged the distance between the pillar and the edge of the desk. Only a couple yards.

Fear coiled her muscles tight. She didn't want to move but she really didn't have a choice and she wasn't going to let Sophie lie there bleeding out all alone. The wound was bad. If she was going to die she deserved the comfort of having someone beside her when she did.

Celida was hunkered down on one knee now, still hidden by the pillar, sidearm in hand as she reported what was happening.

Zoe waited another couple seconds. When no more shots sounded, she dove for the desk.

Crack.

A cry trapped in her throat as a hole punched into the wall inches from where she'd just been. She scrambled behind the desk, lay flat on her stomach as she waited for more rounds to tear through it.

They never came.

Her frantic gaze sought the button Sophie had talked about. With one hand she reached out and slapped her palm against it. A motorized whizzing sound started and through one of the bullet holes in the desk she saw the blinds begin to close.

Immediately she turned to Sophie. The shop owner was barely conscious now, her breaths ragged and shallow, eyes half-closed. "Sophie," she said sharply, needing to get her attention. "Sophie, stay with me."

Those blue eyes focused on her, the blind fear there tearing at Zoe's insides. She tore off the sweater she'd pulled on over her top and pressed it to the wound in Sophie's chest. The blinds stopped moving. They were covered.

For now.

But a terrible sense of foreboding told her it wasn't over yet.

Her fingers were trembling so badly she could barely hold onto it. "She's bleeding bad, Lida," she called out.

"Cops are nearby and an ambulance is on the way," Celida answered, appearing at her side a moment later with her phone to her ear. "Keep pressure on it—Tuck, we've got an active shooter here…"

Zoe listened as her friend relayed the information to Tuck, some small part of her relieved because she knew he'd tell Clay immediately. Clay and Tuck would come for them. If they could just hold on until the cops got here, they'd scare the shooter away. And then Clay and Tuck would be here.

"We're behind cover and the shop owner's been hit in the chest…" Celida trailed off, then cried, "*What*?"

Zoe risked a glance at her, saw the shock and the way Celida's face paled at whatever Tuck had said.

Then it hit her. Maybe this wasn't a random attack. Maybe it was targeted.

The idea made her blood run cold.

Had Clay found out about the shooter before this? Is that why he'd called? Had he somehow found out there was a threat against her and tried to warn her earlier?

Her fears were confirmed when Celida spoke to her. "NSA told Clay they think an enforcer from the Fuentes cartel might be targeting you."

"What?" Impossible. Fuentes had just been transferred to ADX Florence supermax prison in Colorado. She'd read about it in the paper last week.

Celida's mouth was a thin line, her expression tense as she looked around. "We can't stay here. We gotta get out the back before he gets there first."

Terror streaked through her. A Fuentes enforcer was

hunting them. On the move, even now. And their only escape was the back door. "What about Sophie?" The shop owner's head lolled against the wall now, her eyes closed.

Regret in her eyes, Celida shook her head. "We'll carry her out with us. The paramedics are coming for her and we're putting her at further risk by staying here. We have to get out now.*"*

Zoe turned to Sophie, reached down to squeeze one of her cold, limp hands. "Help is coming, Sophie. You have to hang on."

"*Now*, Zoe," Celida ordered.

They had no choice.

Zoe grabbed Sophie under the arms while Celida took her legs. Together they carried her to the back door as fast as they could.

****

Waiting outside the bookstore-coffee shop two doors down from the dress shop, Amanda stiffened the moment she heard the first shot.

Excitement and adrenaline punched through her. It was on. She felt giddy with triumph. *So close now.*

Two people who'd just exited the store stopped beside her, staring toward the dress shop.

"What was that?" the man said to the woman beside him.

Amanda went into proactive mode. "You folks better get back inside," she said, reaching for her pistol. Playing good cop right now was her best chance of ensuring this went down according to plan. "Tell everyone to stay inside until I check it out."

They gasped and hurried back into the bookstore.

She waited a moment for Dom to say something through the earpiece, but he didn't. Not wanting to distract him, Amanda started up the sidewalk.

Another shot rang out.

She paused, unsure why he'd taken another shot. Maybe he'd fired at Celida as well?

The wail of distant sirens reached her, making her pulse skip. She'd known this part of the op would be risky. Nothing to do now but keep going with the plan.

Stay calm. Almost there. You'll be out of here soon enough.

Her heart thudded as she headed for the dress shop. Then Dom fired a third round and Amanda froze. He wouldn't have needed a third shot unless something was wrong already.

Cold seeped through her gut, dread coiling there like a snake. She tapped her earpiece. "Dom, come in."

Nothing.

"*Dom.*"

"The bitch is hiding behind cover instead of going to the back," he snarled.

Dammit. "Is she far enough back from the window for us to use the diversion?" Their getaway hinged on using it.

"Think so. I'm on the move. Can't stay here any longer." He sounded slightly out of breath, as though he was running.

"All right. Stay within range." Pulling back out of sight beneath the darkened awning of another shop, she cast a frantic glance toward the bakery across the street. The sirens were getting closer. They had only minutes left, so they had to act *now*.

Amanda spun away and jogged back up the street, toward the dress shop and turned the corner at the end of the block. Cops—real ones—would be swarming the area within minutes. She had to get around the back and get Zoe immediately. And to pull that off she needed a distraction.

"Do it," she told him. There was a small risk Zoe would die before Amanda could take her, but they didn't have a choice right now.

"You sure?"

"Yes. I'll be at the back in under ten seconds." She was safely out of range now, running for the back alley.

This was the only way to take the heat off them long enough for her to get Zoe.

Amanda steeled her resolve. Everything was riding on her finishing the job. She was going to get Zoe, then Bauer, no matter what it took.

Chapter Nine

Inside the now darkened dress shop they set Sophie down against the back wall. Zoe stayed with her, holding her torso upright. Her pulse was still there, but it was fading, her chest barely moving now.

Celida paused by one side of the door, gestured for Zoe to stay put. Zoe locked her gaze on her friend and held her breath. Was the shooter coming around back for them? Was there more than one?

She looked down at Sophie, lying so still, the metallic scent of her blood making Zoe's already tight stomach roll. Her hands were covered with it.

Pistol at the ready, Celida carefully opened the back door and slid it open a few inches. When nothing happened she pushed it open more, took a quick look outside, then hurried back to lift Sophie's legs again. "We have to move fast," she whispered to Zoe.

Zoe nodded, walked as fast as she could while carrying the unconscious woman. They slipped out the back door and into the back parking lot. It was empty except for three vehicles and a cat eating something next to a Dumpster. In the distance she could hear the approaching wail of sirens.

The back of Zoe's neck prickled. Whoever had shot at them was still out there, would be on the move right now, coming closer with every second. "Which way now?" Zoe whispered.

"North, where Tuck and Clay are coming from. Follow me." Celida closed the door behind them and took off at a jog.

Zoe hurried after her, her muscles already protesting the weight she carried.

They'd only made it a dozen steps when an explosion tore through the night behind them.

A cry locked in Zoe's throat as she flew forward. The force of the blast dropped her to the pavement and knocked the breath from her.

Terror forked through her. She pushed up on her hands, fought to gulp a breath of air into her aching lungs. Acrid smoke singed her nostrils and heat licked at her back. Her elbows and knees stung where they'd scraped the pavement and her ears rang.

Rolling over onto her butt, gasping for breath, she stared in shock at the burning dress shop. The explosion had blown the back door off its hinges and flames flickered in the opening. Above her a cloud of smoke billowed upward.

A knot formed in her throat.

Sophie.

She was lying where they'd dropped her, crumpled on her side like a forgotten doll.

Zoe pushed to her knees, shaky as hell, then ran over to check her pulse.

Nothing. Gone.

Swallowing against the sudden twisting of her stomach, she cast a glance around, looking for Celida.

"Zoe!"

At the sound of her voice, relief made Zoe's legs go weak. She struggled to her feet, ears ringing, and held a hand out for Celida. Her friend was scraped up a bit but otherwise looked okay.

Celida grabbed her, began dragging her away from the burning building. "Run."

The smoke burned her eyes and throat as she hurried to keep up with Celida. Then a female police officer appeared around the corner. She saw them, waved them over. "This way! Hurry!"

Celida gave her a shove toward the officer. "Go with her. I'm going to help lock down the perimeter and call my team in. Get hold of Clay, let him and Tuck know we're all right."

Zoe didn't bother protesting, just nodded and headed for the policewoman on wobbly legs. The shooter. Where was he?

The cop waited for her, reached out and clamped a hand around Zoe's forearm. "Are you all right?"

"Y-yes."

"My patrol car's over this way. Come on."

"There's a sh-shooter here. He's close." She was shaking all over.

"I know, I saw."

Zoe followed her, that horribly familiar sense of numbness already stealing over her. She'd felt exactly like this when that bastard Ruiz had kidnapped her from her apartment in the French Quarter. A psychological protective mechanism.

She tried to shake it off. Couldn't.

They turned the corner and headed toward the sidewalk that ran past the shops. Other police officers were arriving on scene now. Once they reached the sidewalk Zoe looked over her shoulder to see the dress shop. The burning wreckage of what looked like a vehicle sat at the curb in front of the shop, the brick-front of which was a pile of rubble.

Zoe whipped her head around to face forward and swallowed hard. If they'd stayed in there a few seconds longer, she and Celida would be dead right now along with Sophie.

The female cop nodded at two male officers as they passed them. "There's an ambulance about two blocks out," one of them said. "Should be here any minute."

"Thanks," the woman responded, continuing to drag Zoe up the street. She drew her pistol, held it at her side, scanning the area for threats. "I've got a paramedic friend to check you over," she said to Zoe, walking faster.

"I'm fine," Zoe answered, struggling to keep up. She couldn't seem to get her legs back under her and she was panting like she'd just run a marathon.

The officer shot her a sideways glance. "Anyone you need to call right now?"

"Yes, my boyfriend," she gasped out.

Something like triumph flashed in the woman's eyes for a moment, triggering warning bells. "I'll let you make the call from my car."

Then Zoe realized they were moving away from all the first responders. She dug in her heels, resisted as the woman pulled her to an unmarked sedan. A ghost car? Something didn't feel right.

Keeping her hand locked on Zoe's arm, she opened the front passenger door, that pistol still in hand. "Get in."

The abrupt command, the fixed look on her face, made Zoe pause. Instinctively she tried to pull her arm free. The woman gripped harder, her nails digging into Zoe's skin.

Fear sliced through the numbness.

Zoe wrenched her arm back. "Let me go," she ordered. Zoe was the same size as her; she could take this woman in a fight.

The female cop's face darkened ominously. She

didn't let go. And then she raised the weapon and pointed it at Zoe's chest.

Zoe froze. What the hell?

Before she could move the muzzle of the weapon pressed against Zoe's side. The woman's voice a menacing growl. "Shut up and get in, or I'll pull the trigger right here."

Zoe cast a frantic look over her shoulder. In the chaos no one was paying attention to them at all.

Then a familiar figure emerged onto the street, right in front of the dress shop.

"Celida! Help!" The scream tore from her throat.

Her friend whirled around, saw her, but the fake cop delivered a vicious jab to the ribs with the pistol, and Zoe doubled over.

"Get *in*, bitch," she snarled, shoving Zoe into the front passenger seat with surprising strength.

Zoe stumbled forward, caught herself on the center console, the weapon against her side stopping her from lashing out. A bullet there would not only cause severe damage, it might hurt the baby.

The woman crawled in over top of her and slammed the passenger door shut behind her.

Zoe sat up and reached for the handle in a desperate attempt to escape but her kidnapper jammed the muzzle of the pistol back against her side. "You think I'm playing, bitch? I'd love nothing more than to pump you full of holes and watch you bleed out."

Her words made no sense. She was crazy. Zoe had never seen her before in her life. "Let me *go*." Her heart slammed a panicked rhythm against her ribcage.

"Not a fucking chance." Keeping the pistol tight against Zoe's ribs, she wrenched both hands behind Zoe's back, secured them with what sounded like cuffs. A second later she fired up the engine and tore away from the curb.

Helpless, Zoe remained stock still, staring in the side mirror at the chaos of flashing light and running first responders behind them.

Once on the road the woman tapped what must have been an earpiece and began speaking to someone. "I've got her. Meet me at the place in ten minutes." Then she set the weapon in her lap, grabbed a cell phone from her hip pocket, the car veering erratically across their lane as she did so. "Where's your boyfriend?" she barked at Zoe.

Zoe's mouth was too dry to speak. She sat perfectly still while nausea roiled in her belly. Who was this woman? What did she want? Why was she interested in Clay? "I d-don't know," she lied. Zoe didn't want to endanger Clay. Celida had seen them. Maybe she'd be able to get a plate number and track them somehow.

"Bullshit," the woman snapped, her gaze wild as she careened around slower traffic and fled the area. "Where *is* he?" she screamed, the sudden rise in volume making Zoe flinch.

"I don't know! What the hell do you want with me?"

"I want to even the score. I warned you I was coming for you, *Zoe Fox*," she added with a contemptuous sneer.

At the mention of her pen name, all the blood rushed from Zoe's face. *Her*? This unhinged psycho was the stalker who'd been terrorizing her?

"What do you want?" she repeated, her voice rasping in the sudden quiet. Fear was all but choking her now and she fought it hard. Flashes of her previous nightmare bombarded her brain. This couldn't be happening again. Just couldn't.

The woman's nostrils flared in rage, her breathing ragged. "Give me his number right fucking now. You're going to tell him to meet us at the address I give you, and that he has to come alone or I kill you. You say or try anything stupid and I'll make you suffer."

Zoe had no idea why the woman had targeted her,

but she was clearly mentally unstable and meant every word. For now Zoe had to play along, calm her down before she pulled the trigger just for the fun of it.

Zoe gave her the number.

The woman dialed Clay's cell phone then shoved the phone to Zoe's ear. "Talk, bitch."

As Zoe waited for the call to connect, the back of her throat stung with the threat of tears. *Oh, God, Clay, what should I do? I don't know what to do.*

"Bauer."

She drew in a shuddering breath, then answered. "Clay, it's me."

"Zoe?" The raw urgency in his voice sent a rush of tears to her eyes. He already knew. Knew she was in trouble. "Are you all right? Where are you?"

"I'm…" *Scared and trying to be brave, trying to think of a way to protect our baby.* She wanted to put a hand to her belly but couldn't, wouldn't dare do anything to make her pregnancy known and give this crazy bitch another reason to hurt her.

"Zo, *talk* to me."

She swallowed, hard. *Stay calm. You have to stay calm.* "I need you to listen to me very carefully, okay?"

"Tell me where you are." The command held a ragged, pleading note, tearing at her heart.

She drew a deep breath, prayed she would be able to figure out a way out of this without leading him into a trap. For right now though, she had no option but to comply. "A woman is taking me to the address I'm going to give you, and I need you to meet us there right away."

****

More than her words, the tremor in Zoe's voice scared the hell out of Clay. She was terrified, must be at gunpoint or something. The image of her being held hostage again made him see red.

He kept his foot on the accelerator, aware of Tuck staring intently at him as they waited for her to continue. He made sure his voice was calm, as soothing as he could muster at the moment. "I'm listening, raven."

She gave him an address, which he immediately recited to Tuck, who looked it up on his phone. "I've got Tuck with me," he said to reassure her. They both knew it was a trap but there was no way he wasn't going to her.

"She said if you don't come alone...she'll kill me."

Clay's hand clenched around the steering wheel. *Not fucking happening.* "I'll drop Tuck off and come alone. Tell her that."

There was no way in hell he was dropping Tuck anywhere. No fucking way he'd walk into this without backup. He trusted Tuck to keep out of sight.

Zoe did as he said. When she was finished, a terrible silence filled the line.

"I'm coming for you, Zo, right now. I promise, baby, everything's gonna be okay."

"Okay," she whispered back, her fear slicing through him.

God dammit, she'd been taken hostage by an armed woman posing as a *cop.* The woman had to be working with the Fuentes enforcer. Celida was trying to get the plate number now using security camera footage in the area, but by the time they traced it and verified whether it was at the drop-off location or not, it might be too late.

He'd just have to go to the address Zoe had given him, and hope she'd be there waiting.

Tuck held his phone out to show Clay the map he'd pulled up, pointed at the address they needed to get to. "Ten minutes," he murmured.

Clay nodded to let him know he'd heard. "I'll be there to get you in ten minutes." More like eight, at this speed. Tuck began calling someone else.

She drew in a shuddering breath. "I love you."

His stomach clenched hard at the finality in her words. She believed she was saying goodbye.

He refused to accept it. She had too much to live for. They had a baby on the way. He fucking needed her, couldn't live without her.

Guilt was a crushing weight on his sternum. She'd doubted him and what she meant to him, because he hadn't shown it the way she needed him to. Hadn't *proved* it to her in a way she would never question. He'd give anything for the chance to get her back safely, make things right between them.

Struggling to keep the panic eating at him out of his voice, he answered her. "I love you too, and it's gonna be all right. You just hang on and stay strong for me, you hear me? You're the strongest woman I've ever known, Zo, I know you can do this."

Before she could answer the line went dead.

"Fucking *hell*," he snarled, slamming a fist down onto the dashboard. He could hear Tuck speaking urgently to someone, only half-listened, too lost in his fear for Zoe.

Up ahead there was too much traffic.

He jerked the wheel, sped down a side street and blew through a red light to reach the old highway that would take him where he needed to go. The tires squealed as he made the sharp turn and cut across two lanes of traffic to hit the onramp. He and Tuck had their go bags in the backseat.

The woman who'd dared to take Zoe would be down ten seconds after they showed up.

"That was Evers," Tuck said, calm but alert as he reached back and dug out two Glocks, ready to do whatever was necessary to save Zoe. "The other girls are all home safe, so the boys are bringing us backup."

Hell yeah, Clay thought with savage satisfaction.

This bitch was going to find out firsthand the world of pain she'd brought down on herself when she'd made the mistake of targeting the HRT family.

****

Zoe's muscles were tight as wires by the time her kidnapper slowed and turned into an empty warehouse parking lot. They were in an industrial area on the outskirts of downtown. But why? There had to be some kind of trap set here for when Clay and Tuck showed up.

She didn't see any other cars parked behind any of the buildings, and there were no lights here in this section of the lot. Only minutes had passed since she'd talked to Clay, but it felt like hours.

Her skin was cold, her hands clammy and her breathing shallow. The clock in the dash told her Clay would be here within the next few minutes.

Be careful, she silently begged him.

No. Clay was smart and he'd take precautions. He wouldn't knowingly walk into a trap without having a plan, and he'd have Tuck with him. There was no way Clay would come without some kind of backup, wherever Tuck would be hiding.

A former SEAL and a former Delta operator, both coming to save her. She just had to stay alive until they got here.

Except she was starting to get the sickening feeling that *they* were this psycho's real target. Zoe was just a pawn in whatever game this deranged woman had initiated.

The woman tapped her earpiece again. "Where are you?" she demanded angrily. "I'm already here." She kept glancing around every couple seconds, and there was a sheen of sweat on her upper lip.

Zoe risked a glance down at the weapon shoved

against her left ribcage, then back up at her captor's face. Her side throbbed from the repeated jabs of the pistol muzzle, but she barely noticed it under the haze of fear.

She knew time was running out. The woman was cagey now; Zoe could all but smell her desperation and fear as she scanned the parking lot.

"He'll be here in the next few minutes. You need to be set up and ready!"

Cold washed through Zoe. Clay and Tuck were her true targets, and her accomplice was on the way.

She forced the fear aside, focused on what she needed to do. She trusted Clay and Tuck, knew they had the best training in the world. All she had to do was stay alive until they got here.

But there was no way for Zoe to warn them. And if things kept escalating, she might be dead before they even arrived.

Chapter Ten

Amanda could barely keep the fear slicing through her at bay. Her heart pounded so hard she felt sick. She was panting, an invisible fist squeezing around her throat. This wasn't part of the plan. She couldn't take out Bauer alone with her two pistols.

"What do you mean, stall him?" she screeched at Dominic. "What do you expect me to do?" They were stopped in the parking lot, as planned, facing the brick warehouse in the center of the row.

"I only need a few more minutes," he replied, that calm tone scraping over her nerves like razor blades. "Use the woman."

"I'm *going* to." But she had to time this right. Shoot Zoe right as Bauer arrived, dump her, so he saw what she'd done.

She'd heard him say Tucker was with him and even though he'd told Zoe he would drop him off before showing up, she knew in her gut Tucker would be somewhere close by when Bauer arrived.

Somewhere within shooting range.

She swallowed hard. There was no way she could hold her own against two armed HRT members—a former SEAL, with the HRT team leader at that.

She pushed out a shaky breath. "How long?"

Dom didn't answer.

Headlights flashed in her rearview mirror. She stiffened, her hand clenching around the phone. "He's here."

Still no response. Beside her, Zoe tensed and turned her head to see behind them.

"Face forward," Amanda snapped, jamming the pistol into her side.

Stupid bitch. She curled her finger around the trigger. She wanted to shoot her so badly, but couldn't yet. To make killing him easier, Bauer had to see it happen, focus on Zoe rather than himself. And Amanda wasn't willing to die for this.

"*Dom*," she said.

No answer.

In that moment, the awful truth hit her.

He wasn't coming. He'd abandoned her to her fate, was even now running to save his own neck. Amanda was alone, facing Bauer and probably Tucker, and whoever else was coming without backup.

No, she ordered herself as panic choked her. She could still do this.

Carlos would want this bitch to suffer for what she'd done to him. And Amanda had no intention of losing this now. Not when she was on the verge of getting her revenge and her money. A picture of her Caribbean dream house formed in her mind. So clear she could almost feel the warm breeze on her face.

She needed it. She fucking *deserved* it.

The truck was getting closer now.

She was out of time.

Amanda did the only thing she could. She cranked

the wheel hard to the right, then gunned it out of the parking lot.

****

"Hell no," Clay snarled, and tore after the vehicle. He could hear Tuck relaying what was happening to someone over the phone, but his sole focus was keeping that car in sight.

The truck's tires squealed as he peeled across the parking lot and jerked it onto the street in time to see the car veer hard to the left down a side street. The driver had turned the lights off, making it hard to see it.

A mixture of fear and rage tearing through him, Clay used every trick he knew to follow. Up ahead the car veered right around the corner. Clay chased after it, tires squealing as he made the turn, the back end of the truck fishtailing slightly.

Another truck veered out in front of them. Immediately he hit the brakes. The pickup plunged to a sudden stop, the cab rocking.

"Fuck," Clay barked, frustration pulsing through him. The goddamn truck was blocking him from moving around it and Zoe was already a set of lights ahead of them and zigzagging through traffic, gaining distance with every heartbeat.

"Local PD are on it," Tuck told him, phone to his ear. "They've got the plate number and have an APB out. Don't lose them, man." His voice was clipped, urgent.

"I'm fucking trying not to," Clay growled, finally getting enough room to squeeze between the other truck and a small sedan waiting at the light. He edged out into the intersection, ignoring the red light.

Cars squealed to a stop and a cacophony of horns shattered the quiet. He kept his gaze pinned on the car Zoe was in, saw it turn right at the corner two lights up. The engine roared as he pressed down harder on the accelerator, determined not to lose them.

But when he turned the same corner to give chase, the car was nowhere to be seen. "Do you see it?" he demanded.

"No. Fuck," Tuck muttered, looking all around.

A queasy sensation gripped Clay's stomach. No. She couldn't be gone. He wouldn't accept it.

He sped to the next street, scanned right and left. "See it?"

"No."

Dammit! He roared up to the next one. Still didn't see it.

His entire body was drawn tight, ready to snap. He pushed the fear aside. Fear wouldn't help find Zoe. He had to calm down, stay focused.

Tuck's phone rang. He answered immediately, listened for a moment, then relayed to Clay, "Locals just spotted the car six blocks northeast of us. It's heading west right now."

Back toward the freeway.

Mouth pressed into a thin line, Clay hit the brakes and pulled a U-turn amidst more horns and pissed-off drivers, then sped back the way he'd come and took the first right. Whoever had dared to take Zoe was going to pay dearly for it when he got there.

****

Shaking inside, Amanda sped along the darkened road, looking for another place to lure Bauer to her. Driving without headlights at night was plain dangerous but she couldn't think of another way to buy herself more lead time.

The new location had to be quiet, somewhere out of the way, yet close enough to a major road that she wouldn't be trapped if she decided to run again. The panic tearing through her made it hard to think, let alone plan something like this on the fly. Damn Dominic for doing this to her!

She tried calling him on her phone, but it just rang and rang. Out of desperation she tried the earpiece one last time, though she was almost certainly out of range.

No answer.

She slammed a hand onto the steering wheel. "Damn you to hell," she muttered.

Her hands were clammy, her armpits and upper lip damp with cold sweat. Frantically she tried to think of another location. During her initial scouting efforts she'd found another industrial area in a run-down part of town, mostly abandoned.

She swung the car hard to the left, gunned the engine and headed north toward the freeway. Zoe was silent beside her, but Amanda could feel the fear and tension pouring off her. Good. She wanted the bitch to suffer before she died.

Narrowly avoiding two collisions as she merged onto the freeway, she zipped into the fast lane and darted around slower moving cars. Just another three miles to her exit. If she could avoid the cops until then, she might still have a chance at pulling this off.

At her exit she turned off the freeway, toward the run-down section of town. A few blocks down the neighborhood shifted from dilapidated housing to more industrial-type buildings. She turned left, then right, and up ahead the shadowy outlines of the buildings she remembered came into view.

Her heart rate slowed a bit as she gained confidence. She circled the block twice, didn't see any cops or anyone on the sidewalks.

Grabbing her cell phone, she pulled up the number Zoe had given her and shoved the phone back against the bitch's ear. "Give him this address. He's got ten more minutes to find us, or you die."

****

Racing to where the local PD had last spotted the suspect's car, Clay's phone rang. He hit speakerphone, his heart in his throat when he saw the same number as before. "Zoe?"

"Yes."

Thank fucking God. His throat was almost too tight to get the words out. "Are you okay?" He needed to know. It was killing him to think of her wounded and in pain.

"So far," she said in a shaky voice.

A sliver of relief slid through him. Maybe the kidnapper wouldn't harm her. Maybe it was all about luring him there. "Where are you?"

"You need to meet us at this address." Clay could hear the female kidnapper snapping out numbers in the background as Zoe repeated what she said.

He glanced over at Tuck, who was already inputting the address into his phone's GPS. "Got it. I'm coming, baby."

"Clay, just *please*—"

The line went dead.

Squeezing the steering wheel so hard his hands ached, he expelled a huge breath and followed the directions Tuck gave him, sending him back to the freeway.

He didn't speak while Tuck relayed the update to the cops. His mind was on Zoe and what might be happening to her, each thought worse than the last.

****

This had to work.

Amanda's heartbeat thudded hard in her ears as she pulled up behind one of the abandoned warehouses, leaving the engine running. Her mind was spinning out of control, fear threatening to overtake her.

She couldn't allow that. Had to stay sharp, keep a level head. Her target was coming and she'd have only one shot to do this.

Her gaze strayed to the digital dashboard clock. Three more minutes until the deadline. Time seemed to be crawling right now but if she was lucky the cops wouldn't have time to—

Headlights cut through the darkness to her left. She swiveled to face it, squinted to make out the shape of the vehicle as it approached. A pickup.

She swallowed, barely breathing as she watched it come closer. Definitely a pickup. Had to be Bauer. Was he alone, or not?

A sudden burst of doubt and panic slammed into her. Part of her brain shrieked at her to run, to gain more time and distance so she could think more clearly, come up with a more solid plan.

But the logical part of her knew she couldn't run forever. And the cops would be out looking for her in force by now.

She thought of the dream home she'd build on the beach. The crystal clear perfection of the warm turquoise water as it lapped against the sand.

No.

No more running. Her only choice was to kill the bitch now.

It would slow Bauer down, give her time to escape, and maybe even get a few shots off at him. Without killing him, she'd have no money to go on the run with.

She had to find a way. She'd fire a bullet into Zoe's side, open the door and shove her out.

Bauer would stop then. Run for her.

Amanda would take off, fire at him as she drove. Her chances of killing him were small. And this scenario wasn't what she'd planned, what she'd craved. It wouldn't be the same as getting to see Bauer's face fill with horror and grief an instant before he died from a bullet he never saw coming.

But it was her only chance now.

A weird kind of elation twined with the fear, fizzing inside her like champagne now that her mind was made up. A sense of euphoria took hold, filling her veins with warmth.

I can't wait for him to watch you die.

Twisting in her seat, she seized Zoe by the hair and rammed the gun into her side. "Time to say goodbye to your boyfriend, bitch."

Pain exploded through Zoe's scalp, bringing an involuntary rush of tears to her eyes. With her hands bound behind her she had no leverage, couldn't grab for the pistol.

She twisted her wrists frantically, trying to get free. The left cuff was looser than the right, but she couldn't pull her hand through no matter how hard she tried.

Zoe knew she was about to die.

Rage slammed into her, hot and powerful. She'd seen Clay's truck turn into the lot a second ago. He and Tuck would be here in seconds.

This bitch thought she could use her as bait to lure Clay and maybe Tuck to her? Thought she had the right to kidnap and kill her?

Fuck. That. Fuck her.

Zoe fought.

"*No!*"

She lunged forward, using every bit of her strength to twist away from the gun even as she slammed her body into her captor. Her shoulder caught the woman's jaw, hit with a crunch.

Startled, the woman cried out and wrenched away, her foot hitting the gas. Zoe twisted her left hand, hard, gritting her teeth against the pain as the metal bit into her as they accelerated toward the brick wall in front of them.

Zoe didn't stop. Her baby was counting on her.

A second later they hit the wall with a crunch of metal and glass. The airbag punched her in the chest and face. Zoe gasped, winced as the seatbelt cut into her belly and chest, burned across her collarbone.

"You stupid bitch!" The woman's face was a terrifying mask of rage in the glow of the damaged headlights reflecting off the wall. She undid Zoe's seatbelt, shoved her upright in the seat, raised her arm, still holding the gun.

Zoe twisted again and lashed out with her feet this time, trying to kick the weapon out of her grip. The bottom of her left shoe glanced off the woman's hand. Immediately she kicked out with the other, her gaze locked on the muzzle.

Her foot connected with bone. The woman screamed, dropped the weapon onto the seat.

They both dove for it, Zoe twisting to reach behind her, the muscles in her shoulders screaming in protest at the awkward angle. Sweat slicked her palms, her left hand pulling tighter, tighter against the restraining cuff despite the pain—and popped free.

Elation soared inside her. She lunged for the gun. Her fingers touched it. Curled around it and gripped tight just as her captor grabbed it and wrenched it upward. Zoe strained to twist it free, locked her fingers around the woman's and dug her nails in hard to—

Bang!

Chapter Eleven

Clay's heart was in his throat when he leapt out of his truck, the engine still running.

The front end of the car Zoe was in had crumpled under the force of the impact a moment earlier.

Zoe. No, Zoe.

Pistol held in a double-handed grip, he charged toward the vehicle, Tuck at his side.

The front passenger door cracked open but the dome light didn't come on. Someone fell out of the car, hit the pavement. His truck's headlights illuminated a flash of bright red hair.

"*Zoe!*" Her name tore out of him in a roar. He sprinted for her as fast as he could, weapon aimed, ready to fire at the woman in the driver's seat.

Zoe didn't turn toward him, just rolled to her knees, got to her feet and stumbled away from the car.

Relieved she seemed to be mostly okay, he kept his gaze pinned on the open door and ran over. "Zo, get behind cover," he ordered her, placing himself between her and whoever was in the car.

"Think she's d-dead," she said shakily, already backing around the side of the warehouse.

Clay didn't answer. He stopped at the open door, kicked away the Glock that had fallen to the pavement while Tuck ran to the driver's side.

Sure enough, a woman lay slumped down in the driver's seat, resting against the door. Her eyes were open, lips parted, a bullet wound in her right side. He didn't see any explosive vest or remote detonators.

Leaning in while Tuck covered him, he reached over and pressed two fingers beneath the woman's jaw. Her carotid pulse was faint, but it was there.

"Still alive," he said to Tuck, withdrawing his fingers and straightening. *But probably not for long.*

Sirens were already growing louder in the distance. Backup would be here momentarily, although he didn't think they'd need it.

Leaving Tuck to deal with the female perp, he whirled around and raced for Zoe.

He found her huddled in a ball, leaning against the side of the brick building. The sight of her like that broke his heart. "Baby," he whispered.

Clay holstered his weapon, knelt and pulled her into his arms. She grabbed hold of him, held on tight. Behind him he heard the screech of tires, doors slamming and Tuck calling out information to the first responders, but didn't bother looking. All he cared about right now was Zoe.

She shuddered, pressed hard against him. "I'm ok-kay."

He squeezed her tighter, fighting back the sting of tears. This woman was his life, meant more to him than anything. To come so close to losing her—for the second time in just over a year—was too much. "I let you down," he rasped out. He'd promised to never let her down, and he had. It tore him up.

"No," she whispered in a pained voice, curling into him harder, her grip fierce in spite of her shaking. "Never."

Clay squeezed his eyes shut and hugged her as tight as he dared, unable to forgive himself. He should have pushed harder to find the stalker. Should have gone with her and Celida to get the damn dresses fitted.

Before he could say anything else, she leaned back. "She's w-working with someone else," she blurted, her tone urgent, those beautiful golden eyes full of fear. "I h-heard her talking to him. Dom."

Probably the shooter. "Okay."

She shook her head, eyes wild. "You're not safe. They're after *y-you*."

Not just him. Any of the guys, including Tuck. "I know, we got a tip from Rycroft. I tried to call you—"

"I was calling you back when they took a shot at us through the window."

Tuck walked up beside them and hunkered down next to Zoe. "Hey, Zozo. Glad you're okay, sweetheart. Let me get these things off you." He began jimmying the lock on the handcuffs.

Zoe hitched in a breath, twisted to look back at her cousin. "Is she dead?"

"No, but I doubt she'll make it. Medics are with her now."

"I didn't mean to. Was just t-trying to get the gun from her." She shuddered, gulped in a breath of air, shaking all over. She looked up at Clay. "I pulled the trigger."

He stroked the hair back from her face. "It's okay, baby. You didn't do anything wrong."

"Didn't mean to kill her," she whispered.

"I know. It's all right." Part of Clay was glad the woman would die for what she'd done, although it meant they wouldn't be able to get any information out of her.

He smoothed another lock of hair back from her pale face, cradled her cheeks in his hands. Her skin was warm, soft. "Do you know her? Recognize her at all?"

She shook her head, the movement stiff and jerky, along with her breathing. "No."

Tuck freed her right wrist and she immediately flung both arms around Clay's neck. Clay wrapped one arm around her back and cradled the back of her head to his chest with his free hand. "I've got you, raven. It's okay now."

Her shoulders jerked and she hitched in a sobbing breath. "God," she whispered against his chest, her arms tightening about his neck. "*God.*"

Throat too tight to answer, Clay lifted her into his arms and stood. Swallowing, he asked, "Are you hurt anywhere?" He'd seen the car hit the building, and it had been hard enough to do damage. He didn't know if she'd been wearing a seatbelt, but—

"The baby," she gasped, wincing.

He stopped walking, his heart seizing. Her face was pinched with worry and pain. "What's wrong?"

She curled into him, one hand going to her abdomen. "The lap belt. I'm having...cramps."

It felt like every drop of blood in his body froze. Was she miscarrying?

Clay glanced up, cast a frantic look around for an ambulance, then ran straight for it. Panic clawed at his insides like razor blades. He'd thought Zoe was safe now, but she might not be out of danger yet if she was bleeding inside, and the baby...

No. Please no.

He'd only known about it for a few days but he was already growing attached to it. If anything happened to it he knew Zoe would be devastated, and the idea of losing his son or daughter because of these sick assholes made his guts churn.

Cradling her close, doing his best not to jar her, Clay ran her over to the ambulance. The paramedics took one look at them and moved into action, pulling a stretcher out of the back and loading her onto it. Clay stayed close, holding her hand while they tended to her, began taking her vitals.

He didn't even hear anyone come up behind him until Celida was standing there next to him, face pinched with worry as she looked at Zoe lying on the stretcher. "Zo. You okay?"

Zoe pulled in a shaky breath and held out a hand for her friend. "Hope so. I'm worried about the baby."

"Oh, honey." Celida bent and kissed her forehead. "I'm sorry I couldn't stop her. When I saw you guys and realized what was happening I was too far away to do anything." She sounded miserable.

"Not your fault." She closed her eyes, took a deep breath and released it slowly. "Just glad that part's over."

"Bauer."

He snapped his head around to see Tuck standing there, waiting.

"The guys are here. And Rycroft sent us more intel."

Clay shook his head. "Not leaving her."

Tuck's expression was full of regret. "DeLuca's called us in. We might be going after the shooter."

Clay hesitated. He didn't want to leave Zoe like this. She'd been through too much, was afraid something had happened to the baby.

Celida reached over and put a hand on his forearm, squeezed. "It's okay, I'll stay with her."

He looked down at Zoe, still torn. She looked so fragile lying there on the stretcher. The second time he'd seen her that way and it shook him even worse this time.

"Go," she told him with a strained smile. "It's all right."

Though he didn't want to leave her for even a

second, he realized there was still an ongoing threat to all of them and he needed to help. Celida would stay with her. He squeezed her hand. "I'll be back as soon as I can."

She nodded, wiped away a tear that escaped the corner of her eye. "I'm okay. The cramping's already better."

He hoped that was true. "Good."

"We're gonna take her to the hospital and get her checked out, just in case," the paramedic told him as he inflated the blood pressure cuff on her upper arm.

"Okay." Clay didn't know if Zoe had just said that to make him feel better, but he smiled at her regardless, needing to reassure her and make her feel calm. "I'm glad it's easing up, but we'll get a doctor to check you over to make sure."

God, he hoped the baby was okay, but the cramping couldn't be a good sign, and all the stress she'd just gone through, combined with the impact…yeah, he'd breathe easier once a doctor saw her.

When she nodded he bent to kiss her softly on the lips. "See you soon. Love you, raven."

"Love you too," she whispered, her voice cracking, face crumpling.

Ah, hell. Leaving her this way when she was on the verge of tears made him feel like shit, but he really needed to make sure everything was locked down. He wanted this threat over with, wanted whoever else was involved in cuffs—or dead—before the night was over.

Clay walked over to Tuck, so tangled up inside he felt like he was being torn apart. "What's up?"

"I sent a picture of the female perp to Rycroft. He called a few minutes later, said he had an ID for her. He can't confirm it officially until the techs send in her fingerprints, but apparently his insider source identified her right away from the picture."

Clay frowned. That was fast. She must have a prior

record then. "Who is she?"

"Amanda Whitaker. Former DEA employee, who got involved with Carlos Ruiz."

Clay's jaw went tight, his hands squeezing into fists. "That motherfucker." Clay had taken the dirty undercover DEA agent out personally in the raid to rescue Zoe and the other female captive outside of New Orleans.

"Yeah. And apparently Miss Whitaker didn't stop there. She got insider info from Ruiz, used it after he was killed and infiltrated the Fuentes cartel. She latched onto Alvarez for a while before we went after him."

The cartel lieutenant had died from one of his own men's grenades during the op. Clay took a certain savage satisfaction in knowing that. "So that's how she knew about the reward money Fuentes offered."

Tuck nodded. "Rycroft figures she still had contacts within the cartel and the DEA, was using them to get intel she needed."

Clay cast a glance over to the busted-up car where other FBI agents were processing the scene. He shook his head once, fury burning inside him all over again. "Where are the guys?" he asked Tuck.

"Over there." He nodded toward the end of the first warehouse. "DeLuca's waiting for my call once we're all together."

Clay followed him over, maintaining awareness of their surroundings with every step. He didn't think Whitaker's male accomplice would be suicidal enough to come after them here with all the law enforcement and agents around, but he wasn't betting on it.

One of the team's tactical vehicles was parked outside the perimeter with a bunch of other patrol cars. All the guys were there in their tactical gear, even Vance, with his immobilized arm. They were standing in a group, watching as Clay and Tuck approached.

"How's Zoe?" Cruzie called out.

He couldn't tell them what was happening because then they'd all know about the baby. "Think she's okay. They're taking her in just to be sure."

"That's good."

"Female perp's dead," he told them. "Former DEA employee, hooked up with Ruiz and other people in the Fuentes cartel."

Shocked sounds and faces met his announcement.

"But Zo said she was working with at least one other person. Could be the shooter, and if so, he's still out there, so be aware. I'm gonna check with Rycroft on that, see if he knows anything." He got on his phone and dialed the NSA agent while Tuck called DeLuca.

"Bauer. Zoe all right?" Rycroft asked.

"She's fine," he lied, "but she said Whitaker was talking to someone named Dom. I think it must be our shooter." And he prayed it was just one other person involved in this plot. He wanted this asshole and anyone else involved with the plot caught *tonight*.

"Anything else?"

"According to Celida those were high-power rounds through the window of the shop. Add that in with the ambulance bomb and it tells me this person had training. I'm thinking an enforcer-type."

Who was obviously a hell of a lot smarter than Whitaker and had decided to take off after the bombing rather than risk coming here.

"I'll check with my source and get back to you ASAP. Hang tight."

Clay hung up and nodded at Tuck, who was giving him a questioning look. They were in a secluded enough area so Tuck put his phone on speaker. "We're all here."

"Good," DeLuca answered. "We're waiting for more intel here at the local office, and there's a task force already hunting for the shooter. As of right now you're all on standby." He listed off more instructions, then finished with, "So everybody get in to HQ and get your equipment ready."

Clay opened his mouth to argue, thought better of saying anything in front of the others, and gestured for Tuck's phone. When his buddy handed it over, Clay turned it off speaker and put it to his ear, walking a few steps away for more privacy, and lowering his voice.

"Listen, Zoe's not really okay. The car she was in hit the front of the building and now she's having cramps. They're taking her to the hospital right now. We're not sure if she's miscarrying." Even saying the word filled him with dread.

"Ah, shit, I'm sorry to hear that."

"I need to be with her," he said before DeLuca could continue. Protocol dictated that while on standby, everyone had to be at HQ or whatever base they were being housed at. But this time he just couldn't do it.

"I understand," DeLuca said. "All right, you go to the hospital, but keep your phone on you."

Clay let out a breath of relief. "Thanks."

DeLuca grunted. "Let me know if I can do anything in the meantime."

"I will." He'd just hung up when Rycroft called back.

"Hey," Clay answered. "Anything?"

"Yep. Looks like the shooter's probably Dominic Grande, an up and comer with the Fuentes enforcers. I've activated an APB for him. With every law enforcement agency in the area looking for him, he won't get far."

Good, Clay thought savagely. With any luck he wouldn't go quietly, and would wind up as dead as his female accomplice. As much as he wanted to head out immediately and hunt the fucker down, Clay wanted to be with Zoe more right now. "Thanks, man. Keep me updated."

He hung up and told the guys the news.

Schroder frowned. "Man. Who the hell is this 'inside

source' he's got?"

"Dunno. Don't care, as long as his intel is good." His phone buzzed with an incoming text. Celida. They'd just left to take Zoe to the hospital. "Look, I gotta go."

Tuck slapped him on the shoulder. "Go ahead, man. I'll call you if anything goes down."

"Thanks." He turned and raced for his truck, needing to get to Zoe.

Chapter Twelve

*Z*oe laid a hand against her abdomen and prayed for patience. The agents were just doing their jobs, and they were being nice, but she still wanted them gone. All that mattered to her right now was finding out if the baby was okay or not.

"So she was talking to someone named Dom right before the crash?" the middle-aged agent asked her.

She was propped up slightly in the hospital bed, waiting for a nurse to bring a portable ultrasound machine in to examine her with. If they were able to detect the baby's heartbeat, Zoe would feel a whole lot better. They'd already done an initial exam, found some spotting on her underwear but the cramps seemed to be subsiding now.

The fear wasn't.

"Yes."

It was the second time she'd had to answer that question, while Clay was busy taking care of all the medical paperwork for her. And the cops had already told her they'd be coming by later to take her statement as well.

She understood these agents needed to check her story, make sure she stayed consistent since she had no witnesses about what transpired in the car. Plus this was still an ongoing investigation, because whoever Dom was, he was still out there. Although she just wanted to ensure her baby was okay, she knew she'd have to give her statement anyhow. She'd killed a woman.

She mentally pushed the sickening thought aside. It was too much to think about on top of everything else.

The curtain whipped aside and Clay stood there, his eyebrows crashed together in a fierce frown. He took one look at her, then the FBI agents, and his expression turned murderous. "What the fuck do you think you're doing?" he snarled.

Zoe reached out a hand, grasped his forearm. The muscles beneath her palm were strung taut as cables. "Clay, it's all right."

He didn't look at her, still melting holes through the detectives with his eyes. "It's not all right. They can goddamn wait until you're checked out to question you. I leave you for ten fucking minutes and they swarm you like sharks."

The agent who had been questioning her held up his hands in self-defense, while his partner backed up a step. "We asked Ms. Renard if she'd consent to answering questions while she waited for the doctor to come see her."

"I don't care what she said," Clay fired back. "She's not in any condition to make a statement right now, and she's not talking to you or anyone else until the doctor gives her medical clearance and she's free to go. Now get the hell out."

The first agent shot her an apologetic look. "Sorry, Ms. Renard. Of course we'll wait for your statement." He and his partner exited the curtained-off cubicle and closed the curtains behind them.

Clay immediately turned to her, took the hand on his arm and put his other on the side of her face. "They had no right," he began, but she cut him off.

"It's okay. I had nothing to do but lie here and worry anyhow." She wanted this nightmare over with and behind her, including all the statements and paperwork. She just wanted to know the baby was okay, then go home with Clay and stay in bed for the next week.

At that Clay's expression darkened all over again. He looked at the now closed curtains in exasperation. "Where the hell are the nurses?"

"Busy. This is the emergency ward. There are people in here in way worse shape than me."

He didn't appear mollified by her statement. He dragged the chair in the corner over and sank into it, still holding her hand. She was glad to have him close. Celida had gone back to the scene to help with the investigation once he'd shown up. "So how are you feeling?" he asked.

The baby was her only concern. She couldn't even process the rest of what had happened yet. "Just worried. Cramping's pretty much gone now, but they found a little blood."

Concern flickered in his blue eyes. She knew he hated not being able to do anything to fix this for her. "What did they say?"

"They said it's probably nothing to be too concerned about. I've got mild bruising on my hipbones from where the lap belt caught me when we hit the building, and my neck's a tiny bit sore from the impact. They're bringing an ultrasound in to check the baby." The waiting was making her anxiety worse.

Still looking worried, he nodded and stroked her hair. He was such a big, powerful man, his gentleness undid her.

As she lay there waiting, bits and pieces of what had

happened tonight kept coming back to her, like snapshots on a high-speed slideshow. "So, how bad is this going to be?" she asked him a few moments later.

"What do you mean?"

"What I did." The fingers of her free hand plucked at the thin blanket they'd draped over her. "To her."

"Amanda Whitaker."

She stared at him, fingers stilling. "What?"

"That's her name. Former DEA employee who hooked up with Carlos Ruiz." His voice was flat, anger burning in his blue eyes.

The mention of that name made her feel even colder. She'd thought that whole nightmare in New Orleans was long behind her.

She'd thought wrong.

"What about that Dom person?" she asked.

"Rycroft has a source who identified him as a former Fuentes enforcer. Every law enforcement agency on the eastern seaboard is out looking for him right now."

This…Amanda person had sent a Fuentes enforcer after her? She repressed a shudder.

"They were using you to target us. Apparently Fuentes offered a huge cash reward to anyone who could take one of us out."

Zoe gasped, horror washing through her. "I never even thought…"

"None of us did, and we put the pieces together too late. Anyway, you're not going to be charged with anything, trust me. You did what you had to do to defend yourself, and on top of that you didn't even mean to pull the trigger." He leaned in and kissed her temple, her cheek. "Don't worry about that, okay?"

Zoe nodded, but frowned as she mentally reviewed what had transpired in the car. "In the heat of the moment I wasn't thinking about shooting her. I just wanted to get the gun and somehow hold her off long enough for me to escape. I knew Celida would have police coming after us at least."

He made a rough sound in the back of his throat and bent to rest his forehead against their joined hands. "You did great, baby. I'm just glad you're okay. I was scared out of my fucking mind."

Yes, but the baby...

She didn't say it, because she knew they were both worried as hell something bad had happened. She swallowed. "I know it's only been a couple of days, but..." Her voice caught and she swallowed again. "I really want this baby."

Clay kissed the back of her hand and nodded, his expression tormented. "I know. I do too."

His admission pushed all the emotions she'd been holding back to the surface, putting her perilously close to tears. "You do?"

He stared down at her, those blue eyes full of love and concern. "Yeah, I really do. I love you, and I'm sorry I wasn't more supportive when you first told me."

"I don't blame you for not being thrilled at first. It was a shock."

"Well, I'm ready now. And I'm here for both of you." He slid one of his big hands to her belly and rested it there, fingers splayed out across her abdomen. That protective gesture made her want to cry. The heat of his palm sank into her skin, loosening the knot of anxiety in her gut. He gave her a reassuring smile, so handsome it set off a bittersweet ache inside her. "I'm sure everything'll be okay."

She nodded, mostly because she needed to stay positive and didn't want to say the unthinkable aloud.

Footsteps approached, along with the sound of something being wheeled across the linoleum floor. Clay straightened and a moment later the curtain swished aside to reveal a doctor and nurse with an equipment cart.

The doctor smiled at them. "Ms. Renard? I'm Doctor Fisher. I understand you had a bit of a scare tonight?"

A bit? Yeah, I was kidnapped, held at gunpoint, almost killed and now I could be losing my baby. "Yes," Zoe murmured, thankful the doctor was looking at her and didn't notice the lethal look Clay was giving him.

"And is this your husband?"

A beat of awkward silence followed. "Yes," she answered, because it was easier that way, and because Clay was her husband in every way but under the eyes of the law. "This is Clay."

The doctor nodded at him then continued. "Well the good news is the cramping has stopped and the bleeding was minimal. Your vitals all look fantastic, though of course your blood pressure is a little high right now."

He slipped on some gloves while the nurse prepared what looked like some kind of probe. "You're still not very far along, so a transabdominal ultrasound won't tell us much. We'll use a transvaginal instead."

Zoe moistened her dry lips. "Okay."

Clay sat beside her like a statue, holding her hand tight while the nurse helped get everything ready, but Zoe could tell he was keeping vigil on the proceedings. If either of them did anything he didn't approve of, he'd be all over them.

The nurse handed the doctor a tube of lube and the probe, then pushed the blankets up Zoe's legs and draped a towel over her lower half. Then she left the enclosure.

"Ready?" the doctor asked.

Zoe nodded and willed herself to relax. Her hand tightened on Clay's as the doctor reached underneath the towel to insert the probe. She tensed, not because it hurt, but because she was scared they would find out their baby was dead.

Clay set his free hand on the top of her head, stroked his fingers through her hair. "It'll be okay, Zo."

Fear sliced through her, sharp and raw. She bit down on her lip, held her breath. God, she didn't know what she'd do if the doctor confirmed her fears.

The doctor noticed her distress, because he glanced up at her and gave her an encouraging smile. "Just relax and breathe. This won't take long."

Willing herself to relax, she focused on the ceiling, the strength of Clay's fingers locked around hers. He was solid and strong, like a rock, and she knew he wasn't going anywhere, no matter what the outcome. *This* was the man she'd fallen in love with. The protective warrior.

The doctor reached behind him to switch on the device, then adjusted the probe. At first there was nothing but static. Then silence.

The awful, dead sound beat against her eardrums, pounded in her skull.

Oh my God, it's dead. My baby is dead.

She knew it was Clay's too, not just hers, but it was growing inside her. She'd caused the accident tonight so she felt like this was her fault. The baby had depended on her protecting and taking care of it, and she'd *failed*.

Her throat closed up. She couldn't breathe, the guilt smothering her.

Her fingers dug into Clay's hand, every muscle in her body tightening in horror. She shouldn't have crashed the car like that. If not for that lap belt ramming into her abdomen, the baby would still be alive.

Numbness and grief crashed over her, followed by a heavy layer of guilt choking her.

Then, over the roar of blood in her ears, a faint sound registered. A dim whooshing noise.

Fast. Very fast.

Even with her heart pounding the way it was, the rhythm was too fast to be hers.

Her gaze shot to the doctor, who smiled kindly at her. "There it is. Your little one, safe and sound."

At those words, Zoe lost it.

She burst into tears, put her hands over her face and cried, venting all the fear, the guilt and the sorrow. But mainly, relief.

The doctor removed the probe and covered her back up but she barely noticed.

Alive. Their baby was still alive.

Clay wound a powerful arm underneath her to lift her torso up a bit and pulled her into a tight hug, one hand cradling the back of her head. She buried her face in his chest, her hands going to his shoulders.

She clung to him, unable to stop trembling. She was vaguely aware of Clay murmuring something to her, the doctor somewhere in the background saying he'd leave them alone now.

Hard, tight sobs ripped through her, making her chest and throat ache. Her eyes were already swollen.

"It's okay, baby," Clay said softly against her hair. "Everything's all right now." His voice was rough with emotion. "God, I love you so damn much."

Zoe held on and fought to get control. The sobs quieted and the tears dried up, leaving her hitching in little breaths every so often. She leaned into Clay's strength, physically and emotionally exhausted, thankful he was here to bolster her. "I want to go home," she whispered.

"I know you do." He eased her back down against the bed, wiped the tears from her face with his hands and tucked the blankets around her. His smile and the sheen of tears in his eyes filled her heart to bursting. It was more than relief. It was pure joy. "You're okay. And we're gonna have a baby in May."

She smiled back, elated by his reaction. That smile told her everything she needed to know. All her secret worries and insecurities about the baby melted away. It was pretty clear he was already attached to the baby, and maybe even looking forward to being a daddy in a few more months. "I know. Isn't that amazing?"

"Yeah. It is." There was pure awe in his voice. He bent and kissed her, his lips warm and tender on hers. Then he lifted his head. "Hang tight. I'm going to see about springing you outta this joint, so I can take you home."

"Yes. Please." She was dying to go home and unwind with him, rest in his arms and begin the healing process.

He closed the curtain behind him. Zoe lay back against the pillow and rested a hand on her abdomen, feeling warm again for the first time since that first bullet had pierced the shop window.

"You're a fighter, aren't you little one," she whispered to the baby. It would be weeks and weeks until it could hear her, but she knew he or she could understand her just the same. A little smile tugged at her lips, an overwhelming sense of gratitude filling her heart. "Must be in the genes."

****

Clay glanced over at Zoe, asleep against the passenger-side door, and reached over to stroke her hair as he steered the truck into the underground parking. "Zo, wake up. We're home."

He'd gotten to the hospital as soon as humanly possible after meeting with his team. And he didn't plan on leaving her side for the rest of the night unless they got called out to hunt the bastard that had tried to kill her. It was the only thing that could pry him away from her.

She opened her eyes, straightened. He saw the moment when it all came back to her but she relaxed a second later, sent him a small smile. Her strength and resilience amazed him. "It's good to be home."

Zoe loved being at home more than anyone he'd ever

met, so he knew how important it was to bring her here instead of the FBI-designated safe house he'd been considering. She needed the comfort of familiar surroundings and their building was one of the most secure in Northern Virginia.

He'd made absolutely certain no one had followed them here and he'd alerted the security staff to be on guard before they arrived. No one was getting up to their place unannounced.

After parking and shutting off the engine, he hurried around to her side and opened her door for her, then lifted her into his arms.

She pushed at his shoulders. "Don't be ridiculous, put me down. I can walk."

"Nope," Clay said as he hauled her out of the truck and shut the passenger door with his hip. "The doctor said you're supposed to stay off your feet as much as possible and rest tonight."

She linked her hands behind his neck and looked into his face. "He didn't say I wasn't allowed to walk at all."

"*I* say you're not allowed to walk at all." The cramping and spotting might have stopped but he wasn't taking any chances with her or the baby.

He was not to be messed with right now. He'd come too close to losing the most precious thing in the world to him tonight. Taking care of Zoe was his top priority right now.

She huffed out a reluctant chuckle and settled against his chest, laid her head on his shoulder. It felt good to hold her this way, to be able to give her physical comfort. She might think he was being overprotective right now but he didn't care. After tonight she'd be lucky if he let her stand up at all for the next few days.

"Well, I do love it when you get all alpha and romantic with me," she murmured.

"Perfect. Let's go with that."

Smothering a laugh, she rested quietly in his arms as they entered the stairwell. He was glad she seemed to be in good spirits. Finding out the baby was okay had lifted a huge weight off him, so he could only imagine it was probably even more so for her. He was going to spend the rest of the night giving her TLC, showing her with actions how much he loved her.

Through the window of the stairwell door, one of their neighbors saw them coming. Mrs. Flannigan's wrinkled face filled with alarm when she saw Clay carrying Zoe, and pushed the door open for them. "Is she—"

"She's okay," Clay answered. "Had a little scare tonight, that's all, and I want her off her feet for a while."

"Oh, you poor dear," Mrs. Flannigan said to Zoe, hurrying to get her walker out of their way. "Can I do anything?"

"No," Zoe said, "but thanks." She smiled up at him. "We're having a baby."

"A baby!" A huge smile wreathed her face. "That's so lovely to hear, congratulations! Here, let me, dear." She nudged her walker forward to call the elevator for them, nearly fell when she tried to get out of their way.

Clay swung the arm around Zoe's shoulders out to steady the old gal. "Careful there. I don't want to have to carry the both of you upstairs."

"Actually, I bet you'd like it, Mrs. F," Zoe told her, a wicked smile on her face. "His muscles feel so incredible."

"Oh, you," Mrs. Flannigan laughed, making a shooing motion at Zoe, her cheeks turning bright pink. "When's your next book out, by the way? I'm dying to find out what happens to Garret."

Clay stopped and stared at their neighbor with raised eyebrows. Mrs. Flannigan, the head of her church circle, read Zoe's books? Now *he* was the one blushing.

"I'm just about done with his story," Zoe answered. "Should be out in a few months."

Mrs. Flannigan's pale blue eyes filled with glee. "I can't wait."

The elevator dinged.

Their neighbor shuffled her walker backward a few steps to make room. "Well, don't let me keep you, dears." She aimed a sharp look at Clay. "You take good care of her. And she's eating for two, don't forget, so make sure you feed her well." She patted her ample middle. "Had five kids of my own, so I know a thing or two about these things." She waggled her eyebrows at Zoe. "Including how fun it is to make them."

Shocked speechless, Clay hurried Zoe into the elevator while she laughed at his expression. "You're so cute when you're embarrassed," she told him.

"I can't even believe what I just heard." Zoe's books were beyond steamy. Not to mention graphic. "I feel a little dirty, thinking about her reading your stuff."

She nuzzled his neck. "Ooh, you know I love it when you get dirty."

He growled and tightened the arm he had around her back. After what she'd been through tonight he completely understood why she'd want to have sex right now, but it wasn't going to happen, no matter how badly they both wanted that physical reassurance. "No sex. The doctor said so. Not for a few days at least."

She sighed, put on a pout. "I know, but I've just been through a traumatic experience and need to physically reaffirm the joys of being alive."

Much as he was dying to give her just that, he couldn't risk it. "Which is why I'm going to pamper you hand and foot," he answered.

She looked intrigued by that. "What's that entail, exactly?"

He kissed her upturned lips. "You not having to lift

a finger for the rest of the night." He hoped longer, but it depended on what happened with the hunt for Grande and whether his team was called out for the arrest. Part of him hoped they would be, because he wanted to be there when they nailed the sonofabitch.

Upstairs in their apartment he settled her on the couch with the quilt decorated with little bats and one of her favorite movies, then went and drew her a bubble bath. When it was ready he carried her into the bathroom, undressed them both and slid into the tub with her. It was a large soaker tub, but it was still a tight squeeze with the both of them in it.

In the water she rested against his chest while he ran a sponge-thing she liked to use over her wet skin. In the quiet he checked over every inch of her and kissed each scrape and abrasion he could see on her soft skin, wishing he could heal the marks with his touch.

He ordered himself not to get aroused while he did it, but the resistance was futile. He'd almost lost her again tonight, her and the baby, and the most primitive part of his brain demanded that he get inside her as soon as humanly possible to ease that deep psychological fear.

The sight and feel of her damp, naked body in his arms had predictable results. By the time he was done washing her, he was rock hard and aching, gritting his teeth every time her lower back rubbed against him.

Zoe shifted in the tub, slid an arm behind her to grasp the length of his erection. He stilled her with a negative grunt and pulled her talented little hand away from him. "None of that."

She made a frustrated sound. "But can't we just—"

"No. No buts." They couldn't, and that was that. Doctor's orders.

He pulled her out of the tub, dried her off, and carried her wrapped in a towel to their bedroom where he laid her down on her side of the king-size bed. She dumped the damp towel on the floor and reached for him when he slid in beside her and drew the covers up around them.

Snuggling against his chest, one thigh draped over his, she sighed and drew her fingertips over the swell of his right pec. Clay buried his face in her hair and inhaled, still shaken, unable to forget that horrible feeling of helplessness when he'd pulled up and watched the car hit the building, then Zoe falling out of the passenger side. He'd been sure she was shot.

"I love you," she murmured. "I knew you'd come rescue me."

He tightened his jaw, still not letting himself off the hook for failing her tonight. "You rescued yourself. I'm just sorry I didn't get there sooner." It was hard to swallow, that he hadn't been able to protect her again.

She was quiet for a minute. "What a surreal night. I almost died, but then we got to hear our baby's heartbeat for the first time." Her voice was filled with awe.

He stroked a hand over her bare lower back. Her skin was so soft, he loved touching her. In spite of the quiet and her being safe, all his senses were heightened somehow, his mind unable to let go of the fact that someone had almost taken her from him tonight.

He'd be lost without her. Wrecked. She was his whole world.

And in the entire year they'd been together he'd never lain beside her like this, hard and aching, without being able to do something about it. Normally he would absolutely have his face buried between her thighs by now, or have his cock deep inside her sweet warmth. Zoe's sex drive was almost as strong as his, one of the reasons they clicked so well together.

The mental images those thoughts evoked made him want to groan. Her needs came first though, and right now she needed comfort. *Non-sexual* comfort. "How are you feeling now?"

"Good. No cramping." Her breath was warm against his neck. She shifted, rubbed those luscious breasts against him and he clamped his hands on her hips to still her.

But he couldn't stop from kissing her. The primal need to touch her all over, reassure himself that she truly was okay, overrode everything else.

Cradling her head in his hands, he tilted her face up to him. "Zoe," he rasped, then took her mouth in a deep, searching kiss.

She slid a hand into his hair, fingers clenching tight as her lips parted. His tongue delved inside to stroke hers, his heart beating wildly as he tasted her.

Hunger roared through him, fueling the possessiveness warring with the need to protect. He gently rolled her to her back, kissed his way down her chin, her neck, breathing in her clean, sweet scent.

A sudden lump formed in his throat. *My precious raven.* What the hell would he have done if he'd lost her? She was the light to his darkness, filling his life with joy and love. She was *everything* and he needed her so much he could never put it into words.

With a soft sound of need she arched her back, pushing her breasts up toward him. He could feel the heat rising beneath her skin. "Touch me," she begged. "I need you to touch me."

He'd meant to comfort and soothe her, not turn her on, but with how revved up he was there was no way he could refuse that plea.

Cupping the soft mounds in his hands, he heard her swift intake of breath, saw her bite her lip in the dimness. Still sore, and a little bigger than normal if he wasn't mistaken. He gentled his hold, spread his fingers out to cradle them and lowered his head to rub his mouth over their softness, one after the other.

Zoe squirmed on the bed, both her hands drawing his

head down. "Please," she whispered.

"All right, baby, I know." Leaning down, he pressed a gentle kiss to the top of each before letting his tongue glide over the hard nipples.

She gasped and lifted up more. "Just…gentle."

He remembered. Right now was all about taking care of her. The way he would for the rest of his life, if she'd have him. Because there was no way he was waiting to make her his forever after this.

Lapping gently at one hard peak, he was rewarded by her tiny cry of pleasure and her fingers digging into his scalp, a silent plea for more. Her skin smelled like the lemon sugar soap he'd used on her in the bath. Reining in the raging need to take her, he worshipped her sensitive flesh with his lips and tongue until she was writhing and pushing his head down her body.

He knew what she wanted, was dying to give it to her. No sex, but they both needed at least this much. The intimacy of him tasting her, pleasuring her with his mouth.

At her belly he paused and rubbed his face against her skin. Her stomach was still flat but soon it would start to swell as their baby grew. A miracle. He pressed kisses along it, played with the dangly bat-shaped belly button piercing she wore, then moved down to the smooth, sweet place between her legs.

Zoe spread her thighs for him, the muscles there already trembling with the force of her need. "Clay…"

He closed his hands around her hips. "Lie still for me, raven. I've got you."

She whimpered but did as he said. The scent of her desire was making his mouth water. Clay bent and kissed that soft, slick flesh, licked tenderly.

"Ah!" Her grip on his hair tightened, the muscles in her thighs and belly pulling taut.

"Shhh," he whispered, splaying a hand over her

abdomen to keep her still. He slid his tongue into her warmth, savoring her taste, reveled in her soft cry and the bite of her nails in his scalp.

I love you, he told her with each caress of his tongue. *Love you so much.*

Pulling his tongue out, he slid it up to caress her clit, all swollen with need. With the tip he drew tiny circles and spirals around it, tender licks alternated with burying his tongue deep inside her warmth while she squirmed in his grip. As she grew hotter he slid his hands up her body to play with her nipples, gently, in consideration of their soreness.

Her moans grew louder, more needy, the change in her breathing telling him she was close.

"Clay, I need—"

"Shhh." He knew exactly what she needed.

He lowered one hand between her thighs to gently ease two fingers partway inside her, carefully stroked her G-spot in time with the rhythm of his tongue, slow and sweet against her clit.

"*Yes*. Baby, don't stop…" Her voice was tight, breathless.

He couldn't stop even if he'd wanted to. She was like a drug and he couldn't get enough of her. The thought of ever having to live without her tore him up inside. She was his, dammit, and his alone. He already had a plan, was going to do it right, surprise her as soon as everything settled down.

His cock throbbed, his arousal level so high he felt light-headed. Zoe cried out, her inner muscles contracting around his fingers as her orgasm hit. She never held back with him in bed, totally uninhibited in her response, always letting him know what she wanted and needed, giving as much as she took.

He groaned as she came for him, sweet and perfect against his tongue and fingers, waited until she relaxed before lifting his head, his fingers still partway inside her.

Zoe opened her eyes, rolled her head on the pillow to stare down at him, satisfaction and love glowing in her gaze. "I needed that," she said on a contented sigh.

"Me too."

One side of her mouth lifted. "But I'm not done yet."

He started to shake his head. He wanted inside her so bad, but... Right now he wanted to hold her tight, stroke her hair while she fell asleep. She was always so giving with him, in and out of bed. She deserved the same from him and he wanted to show her that her needs came before his. "We can't."

"I know. So come up here and straddle me instead." She licked her lips, her gaze sliding down to his aching cock, and he repressed a shudder.

"Zo..." He was dying for what she was offering, to forge that most intimate connection with her. And she knew it.

"Come up here," she repeated, her eyes pleading. "I'm hungry for you, too."

When he hesitated for a second, she grew impatient. Sitting up, she reached for his hips and tried to drag him upward.

He automatically grabbed her wrists to still her. "Lie down."

Her golden eyes glowed up at him in the dimness. Cat eyes. Sultry and mysterious. "Then come up here and let me taste you."

God help him, he couldn't say no. Not when she'd almost been taken from him tonight. Not when he knew she craved claiming him this way.

Heart pounding against his ribs, cock so hard it hurt, he slid a thigh across her body and settled on his knees above her, straddling her chest. He was still holding her hands, but that didn't stop her from raising her head with a hungry little hum in the back of her throat, her soft lips brushing across the sensitive crown of his erection.

"You know what I want," she whispered against the soft skin.

Yeah, he did. A show of dominance, because it turned her on to surrender to him. *And because she knew he craved it as much as she did.*

Hell.

He transferred both her wrists to one hand, held them above her head in a gentle but firm grip, then reached down to grip the base of his erection. Zoe lowered her head to the pillow and licked her lips once more as she waited, her gaze riveted on his cock.

This was way more than just physical, for both of them. Clay could see the same wild, desperate need he felt to connect this way reflected in her gaze when she looked up at him.

Unable to stand it a moment longer, he gave her what they both wanted and guided the head to her waiting mouth. Those soft, luscious lips parted around the crown, her tongue darting out to tease him.

Clay sucked in a breath, his entire body going taut. It was so fucking hot, how she enjoyed sucking him off, but this time even more so because of how amped up he was. He was driven by the need to mark his woman, take the pleasure she so freely offered, and be claimed by her in turn.

Because the surrender went both ways. He was hers, every part of him, the good and the bad, for better or worse.

But something felt off. He loved exerting his control during sex but right now this position felt fundamentally wrong. He wanted to give, not take.

Releasing her wrists, he eased from her mouth and turned so that he was sitting with his back against the headboard, her head in his lap.

Zoe rested her cheek on his thigh and took him back

into her mouth. His hips lifted when her lips closed around him, a rough groan tearing from his chest. He cradled her head in his hands, caressed her hair and scalp the way he knew she loved.

The soft swirl of her tongue nearly undid him. He lifted his hips a little more, pressing deeper into her mouth.

Scalding pleasure blasted through him. His head dropped back on a deep moan, all his muscles trembling. God, she destroyed him like this. So sexy, so open and giving.

Lifting his head, he forced his eyes open and watched as she sucked at him. Slow, luxurious pulls of her mouth, erotic swirls of her tongue, her cat-eyes drinking in his every reaction, her love and need for him reflected in her gaze.

Clay let her see what she did to him, let the pleasure wash through his system, fill him up until the need to come beat at him with every heartbeat. A tender unraveling.

"God, Zo," he gritted out. His heart was pounding out of control. "More, baby. Swallow me."

Holding his gaze, she took him deeper. Swallowed. And he was done for.

Release punched through him, hard and fast. Hands fisting her hair he let out a throttled roar, threw his head back and savored every second of sweet ecstasy she gave him with each pull of her mouth. When the pulses faded at last he was weak, trembling all over.

Panting for breath, he sagged back against the headboard, gently cupped her jaw as he withdrew from her mouth then shimmied down onto his back to pull her atop him. She made a murmuring sound and wound her arms around him, melted under the kiss he gave her.

He kissed her deep and slow, tasting both of them, the driving need to imprint himself on her still powerful.

She was so damn strong and loving, and all his.

Gonna make you mine forever soon, raven.

But he didn't want to spoil the surprise he had planned.

After a few minutes kissing all over her face, he lowered his head to the pillow and looked at her. Her eyes were drowsy now, her expression telling him she was more than satisfied, at least for the moment.

Holding her close like this filled him with awe and gratitude. He knew she'd reach for him again before the night was out though, and a dozen ideas about how he could give her more pleasure played in his head.

"My gorgeous raven," he murmured. He loved her so much it made him ache inside.

A sleepy smile curved her mouth. "My gorgeous hero."

Some hero, he thought in derision. He hadn't done anything to save her tonight, but he was glad she saw him that way. Because he would always do everything he could to protect her.

Rolling to his side, Clay brought her with him, the feel of her naked body snuggled against his soothing the last of the jagged edges of fear inside him. His fingers drifted up and down her silky spine, slid through her long hair. "Sleep now."

"Hmmm." She cuddled closer, kissed his chest. "Love you."

"Love you too. Forever." No one was taking her from him. And no one was ever threatening her safety again.

He held her close as she drifted off, her head resting over the heart she owned completely.

Chapter Thirteen

C lay awoke when his cell started ringing on the bathroom counter where he'd left it earlier.

Zoe sat up but he stayed her with a hand on her shoulder and rolled out of bed, rushed to the bathroom. The caller ID showed DeLuca's number. "Bauer."

"Dominic Grande's barricaded himself in a house just outside Quantico. Cops wounded him twice but he's not going down without a fight."

They never did.

"SWAT's on scene, but if there's a breach, it's going to be us, because he's been labeled a domestic terrorist and Gold Team's currently taking care of business elsewhere. Get to HQ."

Yes. He didn't ask questions. "Be there in ten."

"I've already called Celida. She's heading over to stay with Zoe. Should be there in a few."

Clay appreciated his thoughtfulness. "Thanks, man. See you soon." He hung up and rushed to their walk-in closet to grab his fatigues.

Zoe was sitting up in bed, watching him. "You're being called out?"

"Yeah," he said, quickly getting dressed.

"Is this about tonight?"

This was one of the things that not being married made hard. For security reasons he couldn't tell her certain things about his job, including active investigations or ops. He nodded anyway. "We're going to finish what they started."

She started to get up.

"Don't," he said, striding back to the bed. He made her lay back down, covered her up with the blankets and kissed her softly. "Stay put. Celida's coming to stay with you."

She seemed to calm a little at that. "Grab me my robe?"

He snagged it from the back of the closet door and handed it to her. Fear lurked in her eyes. He smiled at her, cupped her jaw. "Don't, baby. I've got my boys backing me up."

She nodded, blew out a breath. "You be careful."

"Always. Love you." After kissing her once more he left, and sped to base.

In the team room, all the guys were gearing up, except for Vance, who was watching everyone else get ready with a frown on his face, his arm still in the sling. "Sorry I have to sit this one out, boys," he muttered, looking dejected.

"It's all right, man," Tuck told him.

It would be weird going in without Vance, but it had to be done. They'd be working this op with another HRT member named Miller instead. All members trained together regularly, just for this reason. "You gonna hang out on scene?" Clay asked Vance. His flight to Miami with Carmela was just over seven hours from now.

Vance nodded once. "Absolutely. I'll help DeLuca

from the mobile command center."

"Sounds good."

"Team briefing," Tuck announced. "Let's go."

In the conference room DeLuca and other agents informed them of what had gone down so far. Grande was apparently wounded in the abdomen and left shoulder, so it was likely he wouldn't be too mobile. At minimum he had a sniper rifle and maybe some explosives. SWAT was attempting to get eyes inside for them now.

The team reviewed the layout of the house he was holed up in. A one-story rancher in a middle-class neighborhood.

Grande was refusing to talk to negotiators and the worry was he wanted to do a suicide-by-cop if he couldn't make an escape. With those wounds, Clay doubted he'd get very far, if he was able to make the attempt in the first place. But if Grande wanted to die tonight, he'd be more than happy to accommodate the bastard.

They spent the next half hour coming up with various assault plans, covered different contingencies they might face during a breach, divvied up responsibilities and brought Miller up to speed to make up for Vance's absence. All the houses in the immediate area had been cleared already.

"So we go in through this door," Tuck said, tapping the rear door that led out onto a small back deck because it provided them the best cover during approach. "Bauer, you'll take the heavy side of the room with me." He indicated the side with the long wall. "Evers and Blackwell will take the light side, with Cruzie and Schroder coming in to clear the center. Miller brings up the rear. Neighbors have said there's a crawlspace entrance in the laundry room. Trapdoor. He's probably down there."

Everyone nodded.

"Questions?"

No one said anything. Once again someone had targeted one of their own, and the entire team was anxious to take care of business.

Tuck gave a decisive nod. "Okay, let's load up. I want everyone in the trucks for a comms check in five."

The team hustled to follow the order.

****

When the knock came at the door thirty minutes after Clay left, Zoe frowned. Celida had a key to their place, but maybe she'd forgotten it in her haste to get here.

Tying the belt of her robe around her more securely, she swung her legs over the side of the bed and walked out of the bedroom, through the living room and kitchen to the front door. But it wasn't Celida standing in the hallway when she checked through the peephole. It was two men dressed in business suits.

She frowned. "Who is it?"

"Police detectives, ma'am. We'd like to ask you a few questions."

She bit back a groan, having forgotten they'd wanted her statement tonight. Clutching the lapels of the robe to keep it closed tight over her breasts, Zoe licked her lips. "Can I see some ID?"

Both men reached for their badges and held them up where she could see them. They could be fake, though. She'd just been kidnapped by someone posing as a cop, so she wasn't taking any chances. Her pulse drummed in her ears as she stood there, the hardwood floor cold against her bare feet.

"Ma'am?" one of them prompted. "Your security checked us out downstairs. We just need to ask you a few questions."

Still a little unnerved, Zoe slowly opened the door and stepped back. "Come in," she murmured, wishing she had something more substantial on than just a layer of thin satin.

Rather than close the door after the men came inside, she left it open a crack. Maybe she was being paranoid, but right now she felt safer knowing she wasn't locked in here with them, just in case.

The younger one studied her for a moment, must have noticed her disquiet. "We're sorry to disturb you so late, and I can understand why us being here would upset you. Maybe you'd like to go change before we conduct the interview?"

"I'll just grab a blanket," she told him before heading for the red velvet sofa. But as she moved she was careful not to keep her back to them.

It had been like this for her the last time, too, in New Orleans. Months had passed before she was comfortable being around strangers again. When the men kept their distance and sank into the chairs opposite the sofa in a completely nonthreatening manner, she relaxed slightly.

Pulling the bat-and-jack 'o lantern-lap quilt up to her shoulders, she curled up and faced them. The blanket helped, made her feel warmer and more secure. "So, what can I answer for you?"

"We've been to the crime scene already," the older one told her. "Forensics teams are processing the car now, and taking possession of the body."

Zoe hid a flinch at the word *body*, one hand tightening around the fold of the quilt she held to her.

"We know you've already spoken briefly to federal agents earlier, but we need to review what happened for our own records, since we're part of the taskforce working on this case."

Zoe nodded. She'd expected this, but not this late. Clay would be furious when he found out they'd come here at this time of night. She just wanted to get it over with though. She'd get this all cleared up and dealt with tonight, and the interview would help take her mind off the dangerous op Clay was facing. At least for a little while.

The older detective pulled a notepad and pen from one of his suit coat pockets. "Can you tell us what happened, from the beginning?"

Taking a deep breath, Zoe did, starting with what had happened at the dress shop. Her muscles grew tight as she described the shots and what had happened to Sophie, the explosion and the woman she now knew had been named Amanda approaching her in police uniform.

The younger one waited until she'd gone through the car chase, the crash into the building and Zoe shooting Amanda. "If your hands were cuffed behind you, how did you get the gun?"

"The left one was loose. I managed to pull it free." Lifting a hand, she showed them the marks and bruises discoloring her wrists where she'd struggled to free them from the metal.

The older detective was scribbling down notes while the younger one kept asking questions. "And describe for us again what happened with the gun. How you were holding it when the shot went off."

They were checking to see if she was lying about the shooting being an accident.

The unease she'd managed to hold at bay so far began trickling into her consciousness, growing stronger by the second. *Stupid*, she told herself. *You did nothing wrong and you know it.*

But she'd never taken a life before, except for in the pages of her books, and it didn't sit well with her conscience. Even if she knew in her gut that she would have died had she not shot Amanda.

At that thought all the emotions she'd been holding in check rushed to the surface. It was like she was reliving it all over again, the memory and sensations of it all spinning through her mind in rapid succession. She drew the blanket tighter around her, tried to force the images from her mind.

Struggling to win that fight, Zoe nodded to the detective, described in detail the struggle for the weapon and the moment of shock when the shot had gone off. "I was just trying to disarm her. I wanted to get the gun away from her, get out of the car and run. That's all."

But the younger detective was frowning, and her paranoid brain wondered if he still didn't believe her. "Yet you managed to take possession of the weapon, pull the trigger and hit her in the side with one shot."

Her spine went rigid. A rush of anger surged through her as the implication of his words hit home. Were these guys seriously thinking about maybe pinning a murder charge on her after everything that had happened?

Zoe raised her chin, staring back at them defiantly.

Oh, *hell* no.

****

The team drove to the target house in two groups in both HRT tactical vehicles. Local agents and cops had already formed a secure perimeter and were waiting for them.

When they arrived at the mobile command center DeLuca was already there with the SAC. Someone had managed to patch into the home's security system, giving them a live feed of what was going on inside.

Unfortunately only the camera in the kitchen was working, which didn't help them much. Except to prove Grande wasn't in that room.

Clay filed out of the mobile command center with the others and settled in to wait. Twenty minutes later DeLuca opened the door and whistled. "We're up."

Tuck started giving orders. Within minutes they

were lined up alongside the neighbor's seven-foot-high cedar fence. SWAT was providing backup, holding the perimeter around the target house and patched into their comms.

Clay lined up behind Tuck. A firm hand landed on his shoulder, signaling that Blackwell was in position behind him. He squeezed Tuck's shoulder once, alerting him that the team was ready to rock.

Tuck waved them forward and together they crept around the end of the fence and onto the target house back lawn. SWAT had already disabled the security lights. They moved silently toward the back of the house and stopped to the left side of the door they'd use.

They waited in place for a few moments, then DeLuca's voice came through their comms. "Still no visible movement. You're good to go."

Clay gripped his M4, butt to his shoulder. His heart rate was steady, his respiration normal, his mind and body locked in op mode.

But underneath it was the knowledge that the man who'd tried to kill Zoe was somewhere inside that house. He wanted closure, whether it came with an arrest, or with a dead body. That decision was up to Grande.

Tuck murmured the order. "Execute."

Blackwell stepped past him to ram the door open with the breaching tool.

The second it swung open Tuck tossed in a flash bang and surged through it to the left. The stun grenade exploded in a burst of noise and light as Clay rushed in behind his team leader, Blackwell and Evers taking the right side. The beams of the tactical lights on their weapons lit the room up.

"Clear," Tuck announced.

"Clear," Blackwell echoed from the right.

"Got you guys on camera," DeLuca told them. "Still no visible movement on our end."

A warning tingle started up in Clay's gut. Things had gone smoothly so far. Far too smoothly. It made him edgy.

After clearing the back of the house they moved to the other end, toward the laundry room. At the front door they found a trail of blood leading in the same direction. "Got a blood trail," Tuck murmured.

Clay kept checking around them as they moved, but most of his attention was on the laundry room doorway. Their boots were nearly soundless on the laminate floor as they crept toward the doorway.

Then the beam of Clay's tac light caught on something. Something thin, shining silver in the bright light.

Shit.

Instantly he grabbed Tuck's shoulder to stop him from going forward. One more step and it might have been ugly.

"Trip wire," he murmured.

The entire team froze as everyone focused on the nearly invisible booby-trap barring their way from the barricaded suspect waiting somewhere in the house to kill them.

Chapter Fourteen

F uck this. She wasn't guilty of anything but defending herself.

Resentment burned through Zoe, wiping away the shaky feeling the vivid memories had brought on. Narrowing her gaze, she shook her head slowly at the younger detective. "It wasn't premeditated, it was self-defense, pure and simple."

He inclined his head, put on a reassuring smile that did nothing to defuse her anger. "We're just trying to get the facts down. There were no witnesses in the car, just you. We need your story for our records."

Meaning it was her word against whatever evidence they found.

More annoyance snaked through her, feeding the sense of outrage. Screw this, she ordered herself. And she didn't need to bother calling a lawyer because she'd fucking *been* one up until not too long ago, and besides, she was the victim here.

"And the evidence your forensics teams find will verify what I just told you," she told him, a bite to her voice this time. This was bullshit and the last thing she needed right now on top of everything she'd been through tonight. "In case you weren't aware, I used to be a lawyer. I know how this works."

Now the older one looked up at her. "We know you do." His tone suggested that's exactly why they were paying close attention to every detail she told them. As if they were suspicious that she would try and manipulate the facts to make herself look innocent.

It infuriated her.

"So then you'll know that in a clear case of self-defense, the law dictates that once the police rule it the same, no charges will be brought forward. In my case they won't need a judge or DA to dismiss any pending charges, because there were never any charges against me to begin with." She would never wind up in court in a case like this. Not with the evidence to back up her statement.

A sharp knock at the door made her gaze jerk toward it.

Celida stepped inside the open door and closed it behind her, her gaze going from Zoe to the detectives. She must have seen how upset Zoe was, because her gray eyes chilled to ice as she stared at them. "Didn't know you guys were coming tonight. Sorry I'm late."

She strode forward like she owned the place, held up her badge. "Special Agent Celida Morales. And you gentlemen are?" She put the badge away and folded her arms across her chest.

"Just finishing up," Zoe answered for them. "They decided to question me now, saving me the trip into town in the morning." She put on a tight smile. "Wasn't that thoughtful of them?"

The younger one's mouth quirked in a semblance of a smile at the edge to her words. "We just want this wrapped up as soon as possible. Once the forensics and autopsy reports are in we'll be able to tell more, and clear you of everything if your story matches the evidence."

"It will," she told him coldly. They were doing their jobs, but considering all that had happened to her, they were totally insensitive asshats who could have handled this a thousand times better. They'd upset her all over again and Zoe wanted them gone. "Is there anything else? It's been a hell of a long night and I'd just as soon get back to bed now." *You pricks.*

"We understand," the younger one said. He glanced at his partner and raised his eyebrows in silent question.

The partner nodded. "I think we've covered everything. If we need more, we'll be in touch." He set his card on the coffee table in front of Zoe, began to rise.

"You'll want my statement too before you leave," Celida added, "since I was the one with her when the shooting happened at the dress shop. I was also there when the car bomb went off, and I saw Amanda Whitaker take her at gunpoint."

The two men glanced at each other, then the older one sat down. "Sure."

"You go on to bed, hon," Celida said without looking at her, still pinning the men with that cold gray stare. "I'll finish up with these guys and show them out." Her tone made it clear she couldn't wait to see the back of them, would tear into them once Zoe had left the room.

Zoe had never loved her more.

"Thanks." Part of her wanted to stay and watch, but she was exhausted and wanted to be alone for a while. Zoe rose and retreated to her room, shutting the door tight. Celida would come talk to her when she was done and fill her in on all the details of how she'd verbally annihilated the detectives.

The thought made her feel slightly better, but not much. Now she was wide awake, everything they'd dredged back up fresh in her mind.

She crawled into bed and pulled the covers up,

Clay's spicy scent rising from the sheets. Her thoughts and emotions were all jumbled up, leaving her feeling battered and bruised on the inside. And Clay was still out there right now with Tuck and the others, all of them putting themselves in danger once again while they went after the shooter.

She loved him and knew what being on the HRT meant to him, but man, sometimes she hated his job.

Pulling his pillow to her chest, she hugged it close, and breathed in his familiar, comforting scent as she stared into the darkness.

****

No one moved as the team waited for them to assess this newest threat.

Clay and Tuck edged closer to the trip wire, watching carefully for any other surprises Grande might have left for them. Judging by the size of the bloodstains on the floor beneath the trip wire, Grande had spent at least a few minutes here while he rigged it up.

Using his tac light Clay leaned around the doorframe, followed the wire up to where it attached to the pin of a frag grenade. After Tuck checked the other end and they verified it was the only weapon involved, Clay unhooked it, careful not to disturb the pin, and set it aside on the floor.

"Clear," he whispered.

"Clear," Tuck echoed.

As a unit they started forward again.

The blood trail thinned out now, led toward the laundry room, ending where a rug had been shoved to the side. Tuck shone his tac light on the floor, illuminating the trap door with its metal-ring handle. He and Clay crouched down, and sure enough, more wires crisscrossed the top of it.

"More wires," Tuck whispered, then he and Clay set about untangling the mess.

Clay didn't like sitting outside the trapdoor like this when their armed suspect was holed up below, but there was no way around it. All the grenades had to be rendered inert before they could attempt to breach the trapdoor.

There were five wires in all. He and Tuck worked quickly to disarm everything, then stepped back and motioned the others forward. But there were likely more surprises waiting on the other side of the trapdoor.

Everyone knew what to do.

Following Tuck's hand signals, they fanned out around the opening, keeping a careful distance from it. If this asshole was still alive down there, he had any number of places he could shoot from and an unknown number of grenades or other booby traps waiting for them. They had to be aware of the angles.

Evers bent down and carefully lifted the handle a fraction of an inch, then waited. Clay checked for wires, saw none, then pulled a flash bang from his vest and stood across the trap door from Tuck, weapon pointed toward the opening. The second Evers lifted that sucker, it was go time.

Tuck looked around the circle, making sure everyone was ready, then gave Evers a sharp nod. "Go."

Evers wrenched the door open and reared back. Shots instantly erupted through the opening, the rounds whizzing past Schroder to bury into the wall behind him. The medic was already diving out of the way as Clay and Tuck tossed in the flash bangs.

Not today, motherfucker, Clay thought as the small explosions went off, pointing the muzzle of his weapon in the direction the shots had come from and fired a controlled burst. Tuck did the same from the opposite side.

Agonized screams came from the crawlspace.

While everyone covered him Tuck quickly checked for more tripwires then dropped down into the crawlspace, Clay right behind him. His boots hit the dusty concrete, a damp, musty smell invading his nose, along with the smells of cordite and blood.

Both of them veered to opposite walls of the crawlspace, and in the beam of his tac light Clay saw their shooter. He was slumped in the far corner, just as they'd expected, a rifle fallen across his lap and a hand pressed to his belly.

The guy was visibly struggling to breathe, had at least three wounds that Clay could see. There was blood on his face and right shoulder. Looked like he'd lost a lot of it.

"FBI. Hands up," Clay barked. He was in front of Tuck now, blocking the other man's view.

The shooter opened his eyes, his face a mask of pain and hate as he stared back at Clay.

Right back at you, motherfucker.

But the guy didn't put his hands up.

His mistake.

"Do it fucking *now!*" Clay took a step toward him, his finger curled around the trigger. This son of a bitch was going *down*.

"I don't see any more wires," Tuck told him. Clay acknowledged with a single nod, never taking his eyes off his target.

The suspect grimaced in pain and began to move his right hand upward, the left pressed to his belly. But then Clay saw the butt of the pistol he'd grabbed, saw him begin to swing it toward his own head.

No way, asshole. You're not getting off that easy. They were taking him in so interrogators could squeeze every last ounce of intel out of him.

Clay fired once, the bullet smashing through the hand holding the pistol.

The suspect's ear-piercing scream of rage and agony was music to Clay's ears.

Clay raced over and kicked the rifle out of his lap, grabbed him roughly by the shoulders and flipped him facedown onto his wounded belly, pinning him there with a knee in the back of his neck. Tuck dropped down and secured his hands behind his back, both Tuck and Clay oblivious of the way he writhed and screamed.

When he was secured, Clay stood and stared down at the shooter, anger and satisfaction crashing through him. This asshole had nearly killed Zoe. Would have killed him and as many of Clay's teammates as possible, given the chance. For fucking *money*.

Hope you burn in hell, he shot at him silently.

He tore his gaze away from the bleeding prisoner, looked back toward the trap door opening where Schroder was waiting, guarding him and Tuck. "He's all yours, Doc," he muttered under his breath, and walked away from the suspect.

It was over. Zoe and the team were safe now.

With those wounds and that amount of blood he'd lost, Clay doubted Grande would make it to the hospital alive. As for him, he would be back in his nice warm bed, holding Zoe naked in his arms long before the sun came up.

The way Clay saw it, it was poetic justice at its best.

Chapter Fifteen

"**D**id you find it?"

"Yes." Zoe hurried toward the bride, bouquet in hand.

Second wedding-related disaster averted. Things usually happened in threes, but not today. Not on her watch.

But after the real near disaster the other night, these wedding hiccups were downright laughable.

Her life had been a whirlwind ever since, filled with interviews with various law enforcement personnel, doctor appointments and pulling off this wedding. She considered it a total miracle that they'd both been able to find replacement dresses this morning, and have them semi-tailored for the ceremony today.

"Here." She handed Celida the flower arrangement that had to weigh ten pounds, and stepped back to admire her friend. "You're the most beautiful bride I've ever seen."

There had never been a moment when Celida and Tuck had considered calling off the wedding. On the contrary; the attack the other night had solidified the need to make it happen as soon as possible.

"You have to say that because you're my best friend."

"Do not. I'm serious. You're breathtaking."

Celida blinked a couple times as though she was getting teary, then narrowed her eyes at Zoe in warning. "Don't you dare make me cry."

"After all the work I put into your eye makeup? Please." Celida's gray eyes practically glowed with the smoky effect of the shadow and liner Zoe had applied. She wound her arms around her best friend's shoulders and hugged her tight. "I love you guys so much. Thank you for giving my cousin the love he deserves. You guys are perfect for each other."

Celida squeezed her once, then pushed her away. "Dammit, you're gonna make me freaking cry. Where's a damn tissue when you need one?" She waved a hand rapidly in front of her face, her lips pressed into a thin line.

"Right here." Zoe pulled one from a box on a table behind her and handed it over.

Celida dabbed at her eyes then blew her nose, glaring at Zoe. "No more mushy stuff."

"It's a wedding, Lida. There's going to be mushy stuff."

She huffed out a breath and muttered, "I don't want to cry in front of everyone."

"Then don't. Leave the crying to me, the hopeless romantic."

Celida smiled fondly at her. "Yeah. Kinda love that about you, by the way."

"Me too," she confessed with a grin.

Just then Taya poked her head in the room, her eyes lighting up when she saw Celida. "Look at you," she breathed. "Tuck's gonna lose it when he sees you." She put a hand to her mouth, as though she might start crying.

Celida laughed. "You guys are a bunch of saps." She smoothed a hand down the filmy white veil she wore over her face. "Am I good to go?"

"Yes," Zoe answered with a smile. "Let's do this."

Outside the bedroom of the little B&B Tuck and Celida had rented out for the occasion, Special Agent Greg Travers stood waiting, a well-built man in his mid-forties. His light blue eyes widened when he saw Celida in her gown. "Holy shit."

Celida snorted. "Thanks, I think."

Travers shook his head quickly, the light catching in the silver starting to encroach into his brown hair. "No, sorry. It's just, I mean *look* at you."

Given that he was used to seeing her in work attire on a daily basis, Zoe wasn't surprised by his reaction. Celida was flat out stunning.

Travers gave her a boyish grin and offered his arm. "Shall we?" Since Celida didn't have any close family, Travers had volunteered to walk her down the aisle.

"Yes." She hooked her arm through his, shot Zoe a confident smile. "Let's go."

While Taya scurried out to take her seat on the back lawn with Schroder, Zoe took up position at the French doors leading to the backyard and waited for the violinist to start up. As the music began, she stepped out into the bright September sunshine. Immediately her gaze sought and locked on Clay, who was standing up front with Tuck.

Her heart rolled over in her chest. James Bond had nothing on her man.

In that tux, Clay was the most mouthwatering thing she'd ever seen in her life. His broad chest and shoulders filled out the fitted jacket to perfection. She'd barely seen him since he left for the op to get Grande the other night and was looking forward to some hardcore, uninterrupted couple time together over the next few days.

She walked slowly up the grassy aisle, oblivious of

the others watching her. His whole team was here, even DeLuca, but she didn't notice any of them, her attention on Clay.

As good as he looked in that tux, he was going to look even better out of it. Now that she'd had a couple days' rest and there was no more cramping or bleeding, the doctor had given them the green light. All systems go.

As soon as they got home tonight, it was *on*.

She gave him a sultry smile that promised a memorable night together later, and his lips quirked in a knowing grin. By the heat in his eyes as he watched her walk toward him, he couldn't wait to get her alone either.

Suit porn, she thought with a mental shiver, her toes curling inside the black pumps decorated with crystal skulls. She couldn't freaking wait.

Halfway up the aisle she managed to tear her eyes off him and give her cousin a warm smile. Tuck looked great too, standing up there waiting for his bride. It was so hard to believe her favorite cousin was marrying her best friend. Now Celida would truly be part of her family. Sometimes it felt too good to be true.

At the front Zoe took her place off to the left and turned to face the French doors. The bridal march began, sweet and a little haunting on the violin, and Celida appeared on Travers's arms. A collective gasp rose up from all the women.

Zoe smiled at her friend as Celida started toward them, her eyes on Tuck. When Zoe snuck a look at her cousin, she blinked back tears when she saw his eyes were damp. Tuck was as tough and as alpha as they came, but he had a big soft spot under all that testosterone and the sight of his bride walking toward him had choked him up.

Travers gave Celida away and placed her hand in Tuck's. The couple stood there smiling at each other for a long moment until the JP began the ceremony.

Zoe held her bouquet of roses in front of her and

watched as they exchanged vows, a little pang hitting her in the chest when Tuck slid the white gold band onto Celida's finger. Somehow she kept from looking at Clay, afraid her expression would give her away.

She wanted this too. Marriage, a sense of permanency with the man she loved. Security for their baby. And she was beginning to wonder if she'd ever get it.

A sudden, crushing sadness threatened to overtake her but she fought it off with pure stubbornness. She was stronger than that.

"I now pronounce you husband and wife," the JP said.

Tuck lifted the veil over Celida's head, took her face in his hands and kissed her long and slow. In answer she tossed her bouquet over one shoulder without looking and wound her arms around her new husband's neck to kiss him back, making everyone laugh.

Whistles and catcalls broke out, but neither Celida nor Tuck seemed to care. Finally they must have remembered they had an audience, because Celida pushed gently at his shoulders and eased back, a supremely pleased smile on her face.

"Ladies and gentlemen, may I present to you Mr. and Mrs. Tucker."

The guests all cheered as Tuck and Celida turned to face everyone, hand-in-hand, and headed back down the aisle. Clay met Zoe at the bottom of the aisle, and offered her his arm.

She took it, smiled up at him, the feel of his thick biceps flexing against her hand making her tummy flutter. "I could just eat you up," she told him.

Hunger flared in his blue eyes like a match strike. "We'll see who eats who later on," he murmured.

Laughing softly, she let him lead her back up the aisle, pushing aside the lingering sadness filtering through her. This was Tuck and Celida's day. Zoe had nothing to be sad about. Hell, a couple days ago she'd almost died at the hands of her kidnapper. She should simply be grateful for being alive, that the baby was okay.

Not pining for something she wanted and might never have.

****

"Okay, seriously, where are you taking me?"

The suspicion in Zoe's voice almost made Clay smile. It was the third time she'd asked him since they'd left the reception and hopped in his truck forty minutes ago.

He should get some sort of award for not stripping her out of that bridesmaid's dress back in the B&B parking lot. The doc had given them clearance to get it on, and he intended to, just as soon as he got them to the fancy hotel he'd secretly booked them into for the next two nights.

He didn't plan on leaving the room the entire stay. Room service, sex and sleep, as much of each as they wanted.

"You'll find out soon enough, stop being so impatient," he answered.

Zoe huffed and settled back against the passenger seat of his truck, cast him a sideways glance. "It's not like you to be all mysterious."

Nope, not unless it had to do with OPSEC or his feelings. But he was getting more and more comfortable spilling his guts to Zoe, and soon he'd be able to tell her things about his job that he couldn't right now. "I thought I'd try something new."

It was the perfect early fall night. Windy and clear except for some light clouds scuttling past the crescent moon hanging in the dark sky. A minute later he passed the sign welcoming them to Fredericksburg.

"What's in Fredericksburg?" she asked.

He could all but hear the wheels in her head turning. That writer brain of hers never shut off. No doubt she was already puzzling it out, trying to put the clues together. "You'll see. Now stop asking questions."

She faced forward once again, stayed quiet while he followed the signs bearing Civil War flags to the historical site. The gates were closed but he'd anticipated that, and parked close to the entrance anyway. They wouldn't be here long.

Zoe raised an eyebrow at him. "A Civil War battlefield?"

"Yep." Before she could ask anything else he climbed out of the truck and went around to open her door. "You'll need this," he told her, shaking out the heavy Victorian cape she loved to wear when the weather got chilly and draping it around her shoulders. "Come on."

She did up the frog at the front of the neck then took his hand, let him help her down. The moonlight illuminated her face, made the bright red hair on the right side of her head glow like fire. "Which way?" she asked.

"Up here." Linking their fingers, he led her around the closed gate and up the trail to where the stone wall sat at the base of the hill, where the Confederates had fired on wave after wave of Union troops during the battle.

Zoe cast him a surprised look as they walked. "I knew you liked history, but not this much."

He shrugged. "Some of it, I do. Only military history though."

"Of course," she murmured with a little smile.

"But I picked this spot for you, not me. Come on."

That seemed to intrigue her. He led her up the path that wound its way to the top of Marye's Heights and into the cemetery there. There were lots of old cemeteries in

Virginia but this one had been close and he'd been here before, so he knew Zoe would love it.

Headstones and other markers covered the crest of the hill. In the center of it near the monument he turned her around and stepped behind her to slip his arms around her waist. Before them at the bottom of the hill lay the river and the old town of Fredericksburg across it, the lights glowing in the darkness.

"This is incredible," she breathed.

Clay's lips twitched. "I had a feeling you'd like it."

"It's just so…creepy and cool and dark, all at the same time."

She said it with the same enjoyment most women would show for diamond jewelry. Just one of the many reasons why he loved his unique raven.

He bent his head to nuzzle the side of her neck, making her shiver. "You warm enough?"

She raised a dark eyebrow. "You're not seriously wanting to fool around out here, are you?"

Grinning, he nipped her soft skin. "I could probably be persuaded."

She shot him a shocked look. "That's so disrespectful, wanting to do me in the middle of a cemetery."

"You'd love it."

She didn't answer, but her saucy smile said it all. She would.

A gust of wind kicked up, carrying some of the first fallen leaves of the season with it. They had the whole hilltop to themselves, and it couldn't have turned out more perfectly. And there was no point in stalling any longer.

"You know I love you, right?"

She nodded and set her hands on his forearms, squeezed. "Yes."

Releasing her, he circled around to stand in front of her. She tilted her head back to gaze up at him. The wind teased a few tendrils of hair at the sides of her face, her golden eyes glowing like amber in the moonlight. God, she was so fucking gorgeous.

Clay took her face in his hands and bent to press his lips to hers. Claiming her mouth.

Zoe made a humming sound and leaned into him, wrapped her arms around his neck. He loved the way she reached for him, the way she never held back in her affection and need for him.

Her lips parted and he delved his tongue into her mouth, caressing softly. Just enough to light the fire. Then he nipped her lower lip and raised his head.

Her eyes smoldered up at him. "Tease."

Oh, he'd tease her plenty later tonight, but not here. He had a blindfold and other props waiting at the hotel room, where he could tie her up and make her beg before he satisfied the need raging in that hot body of hers.

Getting serious, Clay took her hands in his. Then, holding her gaze, he lowered himself to one knee before her.

Surprise flashed across her face. Her breath caught and she stared down at him, unmoving, her hands frozen in his.

"I know I'm not the most romantic guy. I know I can be gruff and moody sometimes. But there's never been a day since we got together that I haven't been grateful to have you at my side."

She blinked rapidly a couple of times, her eyes bright with tears.

He released her right hand to reach into his tux pants pocket and pulled out the black velvet box.

She gasped and put her hand to her chest. "Oh, God, Clay…"

Pulling the top open, he turned it toward her and held it up so she could see the blood garnet he'd had set in a black-filigreed titanium ring. "I love you with everything in me, Zo. I'll always have your back and I'll keep loving you until the day I die. Marry me?"

She pulled her left hand out of his grip, both hands flying up to cover her mouth and nose. When she lowered them a moment later her eyes were wet and her lips trembled ever so slightly.

But that wasn't pure joy on her face. And there was a sadness in her eyes he didn't understand. The first stirrings of unease hit him.

"I don't want you to do this because of the baby," she said in a rough whisper.

His heart squeezed at her admission. He never wanted her to think he'd do that.

He caught her left hand in his, squeezed as he spoke. "I'm not. I'm asking because I want you forever, and it's just a bonus to me that our baby will have the security that comes from both of you taking my name. I've had the stone for a couple months now and I already knew what kind of ring I wanted made. I'd commissioned a jeweler to design something a few weeks back." Long before they'd found out about the baby. "I wanted something as unique and strong as you are, so I had it set in titanium."

A tremulous smile spread across her face. "Really? You've been thinking about this for that long?"

"Longer." He brought her hand to his mouth, kissed her knuckles softly. "So whaddya say, raven? I've already knocked you up. What more do I have to do to get you to make an honest man out of me?"

Laughing, Zoe held out her left hand. "Fine. Put that gorgeous thing on me."

Clay grinned and did exactly that, sliding the ring onto her third finger.

She started to kneel down too, but he stopped her by grabbing her hips. Holding her there, he leaned forward and rested his lips against her abdomen. His eyes stung as he thought of their baby tucked deep inside her, safe and warm.

"I love both of you," he murmured, and pressed a firm kiss there. A vow, to love and protect both of them for the rest of his life.

Zoe slid her hands into his hair, holding him while her fingers stroked gently. "We love you too. Forever."

Swallowing the sudden lump of emotion lodged in his throat, Clay pushed to his feet, got lost in her radiant smile. The woman took his breath away and probably always would.

Cupping her jaw in one hand, he leaned in to kiss her. Her lips were soft and warm against his, opening for the stroke of his tongue, hers caressing just as eagerly.

Before things got out of hand and he was tempted to go back on his word about not taking her here in the middle of the cemetery, he eased back.

Zoe raised her hand to stare at the ring. "Oh, it's so gorgeous," she murmured, admiring it for a moment before smiling up at him, her eyes a little moist again. "This was so romantic and unexpected, I don't even know what to say. Thank you."

"Thank *you*, for saying yes. I didn't know what the hell I'd do if you said no."

Laughing, she wrapped her arms around him and leaned her cheek against his chest. "Like there was ever a chance of that." She sighed, the feel of her warmth and weight resting on him soothing him on the deepest level. "I'm so freaking happy."

"Me too." He'd never dreamed he could feel this way, be this happy. Zoe had made all kinds of miracles happen since she'd come into his life.

She cocked her head and regarded him with those glowing amber eyes, so vivid against the black liner and shadow. "I bet I know how I could make you even happier."

That sounded promising. "Yeah?"

She leaned back to look up at him, that familiar heat in her gaze sending a jolt of arousal through him. "Yeah. Remember the last time we did it in your truck?"

He grinned. "Vaguely." A total lie, it was burned into his memory for all time. That had been one of the hottest things he'd ever experienced in his life, Zoe unable to keep her hands off him until they got home.

One finely arched black brow mocked him. "Oh, really? Well, I guess I'll just have to refresh your memory then. Because there's something I didn't take the time to do then that I want to do to you now. In the worst way," she added in a sultry whisper, sinking her teeth into her scarlet red-painted lip.

A surge of blood rushed to his groin. He'd never looked forward to a drive more. "Is it legal?"

She gave him a saucy smile that made him even harder, the damn tight tux pants strangling his growing erection. "As I'm pretty sure it would qualify as distracted driving on your part, I feel fairly safe in saying…*nope*."

Mentally he was already in his truck and backing out of the parking spot. "Time to go," he blurted.

Laughing, she caught his hand, the edge of his engagement ring pressing into his palm. "Yes."

She was going to be his forever soon, and he couldn't wait.

Together they ran hand in hand, down the hill to where his truck waited.

Chapter Sixteen

Clay stopped his third set of bicep curls when DeLuca walked into the gym and headed straight for him. When the boss came to single you out, it usually wasn't good news.

"Briar just called. Rycroft wants us to drive up and meet the contact he's been using for the Whitaker case."

Clay hid his surprise and lowered the hand weight to the floor. He'd wanted to get back to Zoe after the upcoming team meeting but if there was an ongoing threat to them or Zoe, he wanted to know about it. "Sure, okay."

He threw on a fresh shirt and they took DeLuca's truck up to Fort Meade. In a little over an hour, they arrived at the NSA headquarters there.

Inside the main building, Briar met them in the lobby. She kissed DeLuca, smiled at Clay. "Hey, Bauer."

"Hey," he answered.

"Heard your girl said yes. Congrats."

"Thanks." That had been one hell of a memorable night, for both of them. And tux porn might even be better than suit porn, he thought with a secret smile. Zoe was dealing pretty well with everything that had happened, but he wished he'd been able to be home with her more over the past few days. He didn't want her on her feet too much until the doc declared her totally out of danger for miscarriage.

Briar looked up at DeLuca. "I just found out about this a few hours ago, and though I could tell you, you'd never believe me. I think it's best you guys see this for yourselves."

With that cryptic statement, she turned and walked away.

Clay exchanged a look with DeLuca and followed after her.

They took an elevator down four floors. Deep underground now, Briar used several biometric scanners to get them through the secured doorways and led them to a sealed room at the far end. Rycroft was waiting outside it, arms folded across his chest.

He nodded at him and DeLuca. "Thanks for coming on such short notice." Then to Clay, "I figured you'd want to see my contact in person. He ID'd Whitaker, and he's the reason we found Grande so fast. Far as I can tell, there's no other threat to Zoe's safety, or your team. At least not from the Fuentes cartel," he added with a smile. "But you can question him about that yourself in a minute."

Clay was insanely curious about who this mystery source was.

"We're gonna try and recruit him." Rycroft spared a smile for Briar. "Got a pretty irresistible carrot to dangle in front of him."

"Who is it?" DeLuca asked, glancing at the wide window before them. It was frosted over, so they couldn't see anything, but there was no doubt they were facing some kind of an interrogation room.

"I'll show you."

Clay was aware of Briar moving to stand next to DeLuca, sliding her hand into his. Obviously she thought this was going to be some kind of shock for him.

"You'll be able to see him, but he won't see us," Rycroft said, then hit a button on the wall beside the door and the frosting disappeared.

A lone, sunken figure appeared before them, seated in a chair behind a long, rectangular desk. Short-cropped dark hair, dark eyes.

Recognition flared instantly and his stomach muscles grabbed.

Beside him, DeLuca sucked in a shocked breath. "No fucking way."

Clay stared through the glass, hardly able to believe it himself. He tore his gaze from the prisoner to stare at Rycroft, wondering what the hell was going on. Because this couldn't be real. Clay had to have seen a ghost just now, because he'd watched the man die in front of him three months ago in Miami.

Rycroft's lips curled into a rueful smile. "Looks pretty good for a dead man, huh?"

Clay's gaze snapped back to the prisoner behind the glass. "What the *hell*?" Cruzie had shot the former Fuentes enforcer, then beaten the hell out of him on the deck of that speedboat for taking Marisol. Clay had seen it happen.

Impossible as it seemed, he couldn't deny what he was seeing right now with his own eyes.

Against all odds, Miguel "*el Santo*" Bautista was somehow back from the dead.

****

After waiting alone in the room for a long time, sitting in the hard plastic chair pulled up to the long rectangular table, the door finally opened.

Bautista locked stares with the fit young woman in the business suit who entered the interrogation room and shut the door behind her. Young, maybe mid-to-late twenties, long dark hair, bronze-toned skin. Middle Eastern descent maybe, but mixed with something else. Her eyes were so dark they were nearly black, and they met his unflinchingly. She carried a folder in one hand.

He kept his manacled hands in his lap, was careful to keep his expression neutral as she approached the table and pulled out the chair opposite him. He'd lost count of the number of times someone had questioned him over the past three months. If they thought they could break him by talking him to death, they were wrong.

The Army had taught him how to withstand interrogations far worse than the ones he'd been subjected to by the NSA and other intelligence organizations. Besides, nothing they could do to him would ever be as bad as what he'd already been through, while recovering from his wounds.

The woman across from him regarded him coolly for a few moments. "My name is Briar Jones. I work with Alex Rycroft."

Bautista didn't answer. He was exhausted. The effort of staying upright and alert after such a long, arduous recovery made him tire quickly. But he would never let them know just how tired he was. How badly he wished they'd just let him die instead of forcing him to live.

He was already dead. Inside, anyway. His body was the only thing that refused to accept that.

"Thanks to your cooperation and the intel you gave us, the FBI was able to apprehend Dominic Grande last night."

He stared back at her without reply. Did she expect him to say *you're welcome*? Why had they sent in someone as young as her to do this?

"You've been very helpful. And with your skillset,

you have a lot to offer."

Still he didn't react. He didn't know who this woman was or what she wanted, but if she'd read his file, then she knew he had nothing to offer…except being good at killing.

At that, he was an expert.

Those steady black eyes studied him, not giving anything away. And right then Bautista knew she was an operator, or at least a former operator. Like him. "I have an offer for you." She slid the manila folder across the table toward him, left it closed. "We want to recruit you."

He couldn't have heard her right. "The NSA wants to recruit me," he repeated dully, not believing a word of it. He'd killed many people. None of them innocent, but in the eyes of the law that wouldn't matter because he'd acted as judge, jury and executioner all in one.

And sometimes he'd even enjoyed his work.

The rush. The power that came from meting out the kind of justice the men he'd hunted down deserved. Watching evil men suffer under his blade or his hands had been almost cathartic for him.

He knew he wasn't a good man. He'd killed his victims in cold blood and slept soundly afterward, without any attacks of conscience. But the U.S. government was every bit as ruthless as he'd been. And something told him this woman understood that as well as he did.

Briar nodded in confirmation. "That's right."

Bautista glanced past her to the large mirror behind her. A two-way mirror where an untold number of intelligence officials would be watching every second of this so-called "interview". "Why isn't Rycroft making the offer himself?"

The corner of her mouth quirked up. "Because you and I have…something in common. A shared interest. And I have something Rycroft can't offer you."

He looked back at her, held her gaze for a moment,

trying to figure her out. What was her angle? Everyone had one. What were they after? "What's the offer?"

"A job," she said simply. "We want you to do contract work for us, in exchange for an expunged record."

That surprised him. Mostly it put him on edge. They would offer to wipe his slate clean, after all the murders he'd committed? To put that on the table meant they wanted something big from him. And they wanted it bad.

"Expunged how?" Not completely, for sure. There had to be loopholes. Traps they'd prepared with their legal manipulation.

"That depends on you."

Of course it did. He barely withheld his sardonic smirk. She was being purposely evasive. He'd play. "So, what kind of contract work?"

"To start, we need you to help us find someone."

He was getting tired of the run-around. Just tell him already. "Who?"

Rather than answer, Briar reached out and flipped open the folder.

For a moment Bautista felt his heart seize when he saw the photo of the woman displayed there, disbelief exploding inside him. He jerked his gaze up to Briar's, fighting the simultaneous rush of rage and hope that surged through his body. They were fucking with him. Had to be.

"You remember her," she murmured, her expression giving nothing away.

Of course he remembered her. She was blond in this picture instead of brunette, but the ice blue eyes and facial features were unmistakable.

Julia.

"I know you realize that's not her real name," Briar said softly.

He hadn't realized he'd said it aloud. Shit, he really

had lost his edge.

Schooling his features, he kept his expression carefully blank in spite of how hard his heart was pounding. He had to play this cool, not let the people listening in know how interested he was in what Briar had to say. All this time later, he still didn't know who the woman in the photograph truly was.

She'd lied to him. About a lot of things. Not easy, to fool him, but she'd managed it. He'd fully believed the cover story she'd constructed. His research and background check he'd done on her had confirmed what she'd told him.

He'd been wrong.

And yet, his gut insisted that she'd cared about him on some level. That was the hardest part, knowing she hadn't lied about *everything*.

Why? Why had she done it?

"What *is* her name?" he asked, his voice sounding like gravel.

"Georgia."

He tested the name in his mind. Tried to reconcile it with the woman he'd thought he'd known. His heart beat faster. *Georgia.* "Why do you want to find her?"

"Because she's a friend of mine. A…sister of sorts."

Bautista waited, struggling to hide the tumult of emotions warring inside him.

When he didn't respond or jump at the bait they'd dangled, Briar continued. "She's like me." She paused. "A government-trained assassin."

Shock reverberated through him at the announcement. But so many things about that made sense. How she'd been able to conceal her true identity from him. How she'd been able to act the part she'd chosen for so many months without him finding out the truth, only revealing her true objective and skills at the very end.

He never let people in. Ever.

But you let her in. Though he hadn't been conscious of it at the time, some part of him must have known that they were alike.

More than the bullet wounds that had nearly killed him, wondering if she might have betrayed him, set him up, had hurt the most as he lay dying on that boat.

That look on her face though, when the HRT had captured him…

She'd been kneeling at his side, begging him to hold on, her expression grief stricken, her eyes full of fear and desperation. Throughout the long weeks of agonizing recovery, he'd never been able to get that image out of his head. Some part of him stubbornly clung to the thread of hope that she *had* cared.

"Where did she go?" he rasped out.

"We don't know. She disappeared while the paramedics were working on you and no one's heard from her since. I've used every last one of my resources and still can't locate her. But we think you could draw her out."

His heart rate picked up. Was she in danger? He still felt the need to protect her, no matter what had happened. It was crazy. "Why do you want her?"

"To recruit her, same as you. And…she's at risk."

Someone was threatening her? All his protective instincts, dormant these past few months, suddenly flared back to life. He'd given his life for her that day. Or thought he had. And he'd done it willingly, never expecting that they'd be able to revive him.

But his heart was stubborn. Even though he'd flat-lined twice on the way to the hospital and gone through seven surgeries afterward to repair the damage to his internal organs, he'd somehow hung on.

Then he'd woken up from his medically-induced coma in a maximum-security medical facility, chained to his bed, drugged to just below unconsciousness. Helpless.

Wishing he'd died.

But maybe there was a reason why he hadn't. Maybe *she* was why.

"At risk from what?" he demanded.

"We have reason to believe she's been targeted by dangerous enemies, some of whom you know."

Denial shot through him, swift and powerful. Fuentes's people. The idea of anyone hunting the vibrant, kind woman he'd known was unthinkable. "Explain."

"Recent evidence suggests she's being hunted. But in addition to that, she's also a risk to herself at the moment." Briar paused. "Georgia is on a mission to eliminate whoever's left on her kill list. We're trying to find her before she's successful."

It was hard to wrap his mind around the sweet, kind woman he'd known being able to evade the NSA and hunt down targets. "And why me?"

Briar gave him a smile that didn't reach her eyes. "I think we both know the answer to that."

No. He was too paranoid not to wonder if everything between them had been a carefully constructed lie. "Enlighten me."

Briar exhaled. "You got to her. Once upon a time I knew her well. As well as anyone could know her." She waited a beat. "She tried to save you that day. Put her life in danger to save you. That tells me all I need to know about what you mean to her."

The hope he'd been suppressing expanded into a painful pressure in his chest, all but crushing his bruised heart and lungs. Was it possible that Julia—Georgia—had cared for him that much? He shook his head. *They're manipulating you and you're letting them.* "She disappeared for a reason."

"Because she thought you were dead. Everyone did, until ten days ago. Even Rycroft."

He didn't believe that for a moment, but didn't

bother saying so. "If the NSA can't find her, how do you expect me to?"

Briar's gaze was steady. "She might have hidden her real identity from you, but based on her behavior I know she'd have told you things she's never told anyone else. Not even me. And if she finds out you're still alive and that you're looking for her, I think she'll surface."

She sounded so confident about that.

Bautista thought back to everything Georgia had told him during their time together. If he examined it all carefully enough, maybe there was some hidden clue that would help him find her.

"If you let me out of here and announce that I'm still alive, I won't be for long." He'd made a lot of enemies during his time as Perez's enforcer. Some of them would want revenge. And right now, he was barely able to function. It would be weeks more until he regained even half of his strength.

Briar inclined her head. "You'll have backup. We'll be working together on this."

He wanted to laugh but it would hurt too much. "You and me?"

"Yes, along with whatever NSA resources we need. We'll have to be careful how we make the announcement, and who we announce it to."

If she thought he would jump at the offer, she was mistaken. "What about my grandmother?"

She didn't show any surprise at the sudden change in topic. "She's still in her care facility in Miami."

"I want to see her, talk to her. And she'll need to be moved to a more secure facility. I want her looked after for the rest of her life."

She nodded. "That could all be arranged, provided you sign the contract." She shifted Georgia's picture aside to expose a legal document, and tilted her head. "So you'll do it?"

"I didn't say that." Who knew what terms they'd included in that thing? There was no way they were ever going to let him be a free man again. Not after what he'd done.

"But you'll consider it."

His jaw tightened. They had him exactly where they wanted him, and they knew it. His choices were either to spend the rest of his life rotting away in whatever dark hole they put him in, or play the puppet and face death once more by agreeing to take this op. He'd constantly be on guard against the enemies gunning for him, as well as the people who claimed to be his allies.

He was done with that kind of life. It was why he'd been about to relocate to the Caymans after that last job for Perez in the Keys. Then, within the space of a few hours, everything had gone to hell.

"I'll read the contract," he finally answered.

"Good." Briar stood and headed for the door. "When you make your decision you can let one of the guards know." She exited the room.

Alone, Bautista stared into the mirrored wall before him. People were out there in the hallway, watching him, Rycroft certainly. He didn't care about any of them, more concerned with the reflection staring back at him.

He barely recognized himself. His face was sunken, deep shadows beneath his eyes, the only color in his too-pale face. Even his body, once powerful, was now frail-looking, shrunken in the bright orange prison suit.

He looked…broken.

But he wasn't. Not even close.

Almost against his will his gaze strayed back to the folder on the desk. Georgia's cool blue eyes peered back at the camera, devoid of emotion except for a hint of anger he recognized all too well.

The government had turned her into a weapon, same as it had him. They were merely assets to be exploited by the people who wanted to use them, nothing more.

How strange and ironic, to learn they had far more in common than he'd ever realized. She'd haunted him. Would haunt him forever. The memory of how she'd looked at him, with such trust and admiration. They way she'd touched him, the feel of her lips on his skin, her naked body writhing beneath his.

He stared at the papers. The contract was an opportunity for him to find out whether any of what they'd shared was real. A chance for closure, or…

Maybe even the infinitesimal chance of something more.

Epilogue

Ten weeks later

Clay stared at the swell of Zoe's abdomen as the technician spread some kind of gel over it, beneath the end of the dangly bat belly-button piercing Zoe wore. She'd probably have to take it out in another few months.

His wife's belly was going to get a whole lot bigger before this was over.

It still felt surreal that they were married and having a kid together. They'd wound up eloping at the courthouse on Halloween night, with Tuck and Celida acting as witnesses. His team had been busy as ever these past few months, but the timing had worked out and Clay was glad he'd been able to marry Zoe on her most favorite night of the year.

She gasped, let out a giggle. "That's cold!"

The tech smiled at her. "I know, sorry. But it'll warm up quick. You ready?"

"Ready," she answered with a nod. She reached for

his hand and Clay grabbed it, lacing their fingers together.

Truth was, he was nervous as fuck, and doing his damnedest not to let it show. The doctor had assured them already that there was only one baby in there, but what if he was wrong? What if there were two? And what if it *was* only one, but it only had one eye? Or it was missing part of its brain or something? He'd seen a documentary about that two weeks ago.

He'd had nightmares about it ever since.

"Okay, here we go." The tech set the Doppler against Zoe's abdomen.

Clay's gaze shot to the black and white screen mounted on the wall. At first he saw nothing but a series of indistinguishable lines, but then a fuzzy shape appeared. Something round, then something even bigger and rounder.

Shit, his heart was pounding. He didn't know what the hell he was even looking at, so he had no clue if it was normal or not. He squinted.

The tech moved the device around some more. "Can you shift onto your right side a bit?" she asked Zoe.

Zoe rolled a little and Clay tucked a pillow under her lower back to bolster her. Then Zoe gasped and his gaze darted back to the screen. What? What was happening? Was something wrong?

"Oh…"

Zoe sounded on the verge of tears, and Clay prayed they were happy ones. He held his breath as he stared at the screen, squinting to see whatever it was that had made Zoe so emotional.

Then, out of the fuzzy shadows and lines, a tiny profile appeared. Clay went dead still, unable to look away.

"Oh, Clay, look," Zoe gushed, squeezing his hand tight.

"I see it," he said in an awed voice. A tiny head, a

cute little nose, even an itty-bitty chin. Their baby. He was looking at a picture of their baby.

He hadn't thought he'd get emotional, but the sight of that fragile little being tucked inside Zoe made his throat tighten.

Hey, little fella, he silently told it.

Not it, *him.* Had to be a him, because Clay wasn't sure he could handle the alternative. Constantly worrying about the health and happiness of one female in their house was enough. Adding another one would surely kill him.

The tech smiled and began pointing things out to them. The brain was perfectly intact, thank God, and the other organs appeared to be well-formed. She divided a look between them. "Do you want to know the sex?"

"Yes, please," Zoe said eagerly.

"All right. Baby's being pretty cooperative at the moment, so let's see if we can get a peek." The tech slid the wand lower, to between the baby's legs. Only the baby was turned the wrong way. "Shift a little more to your right side," she told Zoe.

Zoe did, and to Clay's amazement, their baby moved. Its little arms jerked, as if startled by the movement, and its legs shifted apart.

Clay leaned forward, staring hard at the spot between its legs. *Please let there be a penis. Please let there be a penis.*

"Well, Dad?"

It took him a moment to realize the tech was speaking to him. "Huh?"

She laughed. "What do you think? Boy or girl?"

He peered back at the screen. "I don't know, I can't see anything…"

"That's exactly right." She smiled at them both. "Congratulations, it's a little girl."

What? *No way.* Leaning in closer, he squinted hard.

"Are you sure?"

"I'm sure," the tech answered dryly.

"Oh, Clay, it's a girl," Zoe breathed, sounding like she might start crying at any second. If she did he'd lose it. He couldn't stand seeing her cry.

But instead of crying Zoe turned her head to look at him and burst out laughing.

Clay blinked at her reaction. "What?"

"Oh my God, you should see your face. Wait, do it again," she insisted, reaching for her phone and holding it up. "I want a picture to send to Tuck and Celida."

He scowled at her. "No. There's no face."

She giggled at him. "There totally was." She turned to the tech. "My former SEAL husband is freaking out over the thought of being a father to a little girl."

Both of them laughed while Clay sat there and took it, a blush creeping into his cheeks. "I'm not freaking out." SEALs didn't freak out, they dealt with shit.

Ignoring the women, he stared back at the screen, a powerful and unexpected rush of love filling him. It was amazing, seeing her fragile little form inside Zoe.

That's my little girl right there, he thought in awe.

He might not have the first clue what to do with a daughter, but he'd learn. And he'd kick anyone's ass who fucking dared hurt her. On purpose or by accident, it didn't matter. Either way, they were fucked.

"Oh, and I'm well-acquainted with *that* look," Zoe said, snapping a picture. She lowered the phone, a pleased smile on her face. "Just look at that shot, Daddy."

She held up the phone for him, showing the picture. The image startled Clay. He looked fierce as he stared at that first image of his daughter. Like a warrior. Ready to kick ass and keep his little girl safe at all costs.

He looked like a father, ready to protect what was his.

And he would. Always.

Taking pride in both the thought and the image, Clay smiled and leaned over to kiss Zoe's lips, totally unapologetic about his expression in that photo. "Once a SEAL, always a SEAL. And nobody's gonna mess with our baby girl with me around."

—The End—

Thank you for reading WANTED. I really hope you enjoyed it and that you'll consider leaving a review at one of your favorite online retailers. It's a great way to help other readers discover new books.

If you liked WANTED and would like to read more, turn the page for a list of my other books. And if you don't want to miss any future releases, please feel free to join my newsletter: http://kayleacross.com/v2/contact/

Complete Booklist

Romantic Suspense
Hostage Rescue Team Series
Marked
Targeted
Hunted
Disavowed
Avenged
Exposed
Seized
Wanted

Titanium Security Series
Ignited
Singed
Burned
Extinguished
Rekindled

Bagram Special Ops Series
Deadly Descent
Tactical Strike
Lethal Pursuit
Danger Close
Collateral Damage

Suspense Series
Out of Her League
Cover of Darkness
No Turning Back
Relentless
Absolution

Paranormal Romance
Empowered Series
Darkest Caress

Historical Romance
The Vacant Chair

Erotic Romance (writing as *Callie Croix*)
Deacon's Touch
Dillon's Claim
No Holds Barred
Touch Me
Let Me In
Covert Seduction

Acknowledgements

Many thanks to my team for helping me with this story! My editors Deb and Joan, Katie Reus my fabulous critique partner and bestie. And DH, for lending me your eagle eyes.

Couldn't have done this without you guys!

About the Author

NY Times and USA Today Bestselling author Kaylea Cross writes edge-of-your-seat military romantic suspense. Her work has won many awards and has been nominated for both the Daphne du Maurier and the National Readers' Choice Awards. A Registered Massage Therapist by trade, Kaylea is also an avid gardener, artist, Civil War buff, Special Ops aficionado, belly dance enthusiast and former nationally-carded softball pitcher. She lives in Vancouver, BC with her husband and family.

You can visit Kaylea at www.kayleacross.com. If you would like to be notified of future releases, please join her newsletter: http://kayleacross.com/v2/contact/

CPSIA information can be obtained
at www.ICGtesting.com
Printed in the USA
LVHW091611130319
610527LV00001B/115/P